Free Breeze

A Nautical Novel

By
Ed Robinson

Copyright 2015 Ed Robinson
All rights reserved.

This is a work of fiction. Real people and actual places are used fictitiously. Although some of the events described are loosely based on my true life experience, they are mostly products of my imagination.

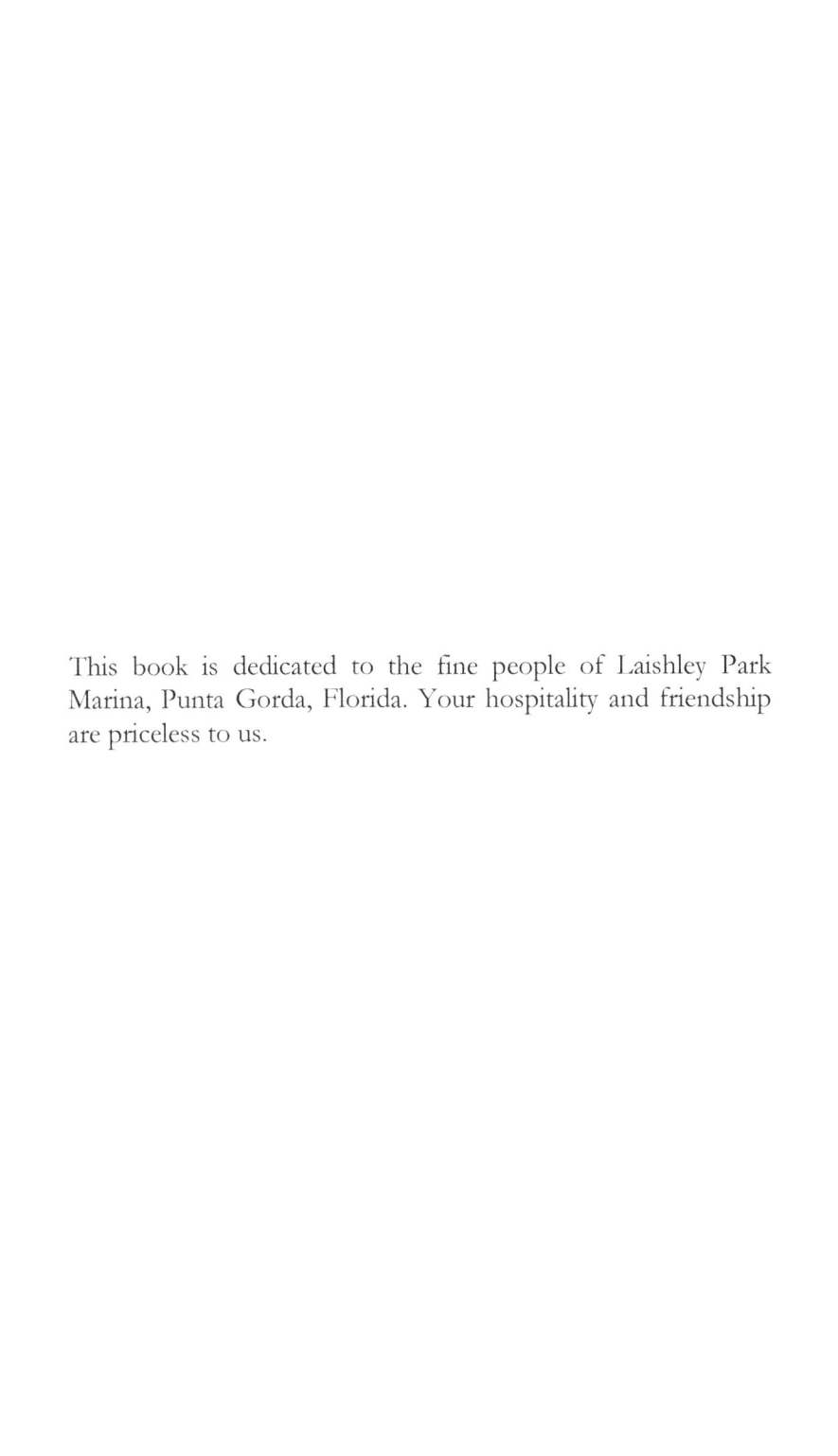

This book is dedicated to the fine people of Laishley Park Marina, Punta Gorda, Florida. Your hospitality and friendship are priceless to us.

Getting Right with the Law

My new digs were in the Kent County Detention Center, in downtown Dover, Delaware. It could have been worse. The Delaware Correctional Center, a real jail, was just up the road in Smyrna. My father had run it with an iron fist for twenty years. I wouldn't have lasted a day.

Instead, they had stashed me in what amounted to a drunk tank, awaiting resolution of my various legal issues. My roommates were harmless. George had recently earned his sixth DUI. He spent weekends in here after his fifth. Still hadn't learned his lesson. Marcus was trying to figure out how he was supposed to pay his back child support while he was locked up. We played gin rummy between lawyer visits and trips to the yard.

My lawyer, Mike Savage, was in negotiations with my former employer over repayment of the money I had stolen from them. The executives of Mid-Atlantic Natural Gas were split on the issue. My old boss, Bob Zola, was pushing for them to accept repayment plus interest, in exchange for dropping the charges. Some of the others wanted me to go to jail.

Meanwhile, the pencil pushers at the IRS were busy compounding interest and piling on penalties for my tax evasion. I had left my cash with Mike, almost half a million dollars. I hoped there would be some left when this was finished.

At night, I'd lie there in the dark and think about Joy. She had promised to wait for me. I thought about Laura too. I didn't have her ashes with me anymore, so I didn't talk to her. Joy was out there somewhere, flirting for drinks. She was still free. I was not. That was the worst part. The place was a minimum security facility, and quite comfortable, but the confinement was killing me. I was far from my boat. I couldn't see any water. I couldn't see the sunset from our window.

Normally, a person like me would qualify for bail. As explained by my lawyer, the pending IRS decision, and ultimately the pot possession charge in Florida, meant that I'd remain in custody until it was all sorted out.

I wasted away for three weeks. Finally, Mike met with me to lay it all out.

"Your old boss has won the day," he said. "Zola got them to take the money. All charges are dropped."

"That's great," I replied. "How much interest did I pay?"

"That's the bad news," he answered. "I was pushing for ten grand, but they wouldn't think of it. Total payback is one-fifty."

"Damn. Sixty grand in interest? I hope you can do better than that with the IRS."

"You better just hope I can get you out of jail," he said. "Don't do the crime, and all that."

"You're right," I said. "When do you meet with the tax people?"

"Tomorrow," he answered. "It's going to cost you. You're not in much of a position to negotiate."

"Just try to leave me with enough to fight the pot charge," I said. "I can survive with no money, but I can't survive in jail."

"I'll do what I can, Breeze," he said. "Don't forget you have to pay me too."

He left me alone to do the math. I was allergic to money. Every time I got in the black, something came along to take it all away from me. Plus, I tended to blow through it pretty quick. Maybe I was better off being broke. The next afternoon, Mike was back.

"You're out another hundred grand," he said. The IRS has accepted full reparations, with interest and ridiculous penalties. There will be no charges of evasion. You're all paid up."

"I just lost a quarter million dollars in two days," I said. "Didn't even get a glass of champagne out of it."

"I'll get you checked out of here in the morning," he said. "I'll buy the champagne, deduct it from the fifty grand you're paying me."

"Staying out of jail is expensive," I said. "But freedom is priceless. Thanks Mike."

The next day, I said my goodbyes to George and Marcus. Mike and I drank champagne straight out of the bottle, in his office. He handed me my briefcase full of cash. It was considerably lighter then when I gave it to him. I thumbed through the bills while he made arrangements for my transfer back to Florida. I had just under two hundred grand left. He'd also lined up an attorney to represent me on the marijuana possession charges. He told me that the judge and prosecutor were arguing behind closed doors about my case. Two pounds was certainly worthy of a charge of intent to distribute, but it was all in one big bale with no paraphernalia. I would tell them that I found it on the beach in an effort to reduce the charges.

I rotted in a cell in Fort Myers for a few days before my new lawyer showed up. When she walked into the conference room,

I was taken aback. She was hot, in a school teacher or librarian sort of way. Her auburn hair hung down around the frames of her glasses and flowed over her shoulders. She wore a tight skirt, which stopped above the knee. Under her businesslike jacket she wore a white, lacy top that looked like lingerie. Her high-heels clacked across the tile floor as she approached the table.

"Mr. Meade Breeze?" she asked.

"Just Breeze if you don't mind," I answered. "Nobody calls me Meade."

I thought of Andi and Yolanda briefly, but turned my attention quickly back to the pretty lady in front of me.

"Taylor Ford," she said, holding out her hand. "I'm the best drug defense attorney in South Florida. I don't come cheap. Do you have the means to pay for my services?"

"That depends," I answered. "What range are we talking about?"

"If we plea out clean and easy, twenty-five grand," she answered. "If we go to trial, upwards of a hundred grand. You're other option is to bribe a judge, I can help you with that if you have the cash. It would help if you had some political connections. We can do wonders with who you know."

She was all business. She made bribing a judge sound like a professional courtesy. She was completely in control of the situation, no nonsense.

"Bribe a judge?" I asked. "Really?"

"This is Lee County, Breeze. Everyone has a price. It's just knowing who to get to at the right time. Do you have any connections at all in local politics? Law enforcement? The business world?"

She sounded doubtful. She had her head down looking at a folder. She raised her eyes to look at me over her glasses, which had fallen down her cute little nose. She had no reason to think that a boat bum like me would know anyone important. Then it hit me. Captain Fred could buy and sell this whole county. He had multiple politicians in his pocket at one time. He built a huge airport in central Florida, which he later sold to the Port of Miami for a zillion dollars. He was the ultimate political animal in these parts, and he was my friend.

"You need to contact Captain Fred. He's on his boat, Incognito, in Georgetown Harbor. He's in the Bahamas, the Exumas to be exact. The harbormaster can contact him, or give you his number. I'm certain he can help."

"Do you mean Cargo Fresh Fred?" she asked. "TWA Fred? Buddies with the Fedex founder Fred? How in the hell do you know him?"

"It's a long story," I said. "But we go way back. If I knew bribery was an option, I'd have turned to him first. There is no one more adept at navigating the seediness of Florida politics than him."

"This is an interesting development, Breeze," she said. "If Fred can push the right buttons, we'll have you free as a bird in no time."

"Any way you can arrange to get me out on bail in the meantime?" I asked.

"Your current judge considers you a flight risk, living on a boat and all," she answered. "Let me contact Fred first. You'll need your cash to pay somebody off, and to pay me."

"Everybody wants what little I've got," I lamented.

"I'm not the one who was caught with two pounds of dope," she replied. "But I am the one who will get you out of a prison term. Let me go work on contacting Fred. I'll be back when I know something worth telling you. Sit tight."

"Like I have a choice," I said. "Thanks for being frank with me. Do what you can."

Once again, a lawyer left me to do the math. I waited three more days wondering what Fred and Taylor would be able to do for me. In my bed at night, I pictured her without clothes. I saw her tight skirt, tailored jacket, and lacy things, in a pile on the floor. She was still wearing her glasses, and high-heels.

I couldn't help but picture her naked again when she walked back into the conference room. The clacking of her heels, snapped me out of it. She was dressed much the same, but in different colors. The lacy top was a pale pink. She plopped a file down on the table, crossed her arms, cocked her hip, and looked me over for a few seconds.

"You are a very interesting character, Breeze," she declared. "Captain Fred thinks the world of you. I had to listen to an hour of stories before we could get down to business."

"That's Fred," I said. "Was he able to provide any help?"

"It took him two days to get to every circuit court judge in the district," she answered. "None of them would ever dare to cross him. He's had your case reassigned to a sympathetic judge with a lot of debt. All I have to do is deliver an envelope full of cash in exchange for leniency."

"How much money, and how much leniency?" I asked.

"You're presented a three-tiered set of options," she began. "For fifty grand, you get a one year sentence, serving three months."

"Unacceptable," I said.

"For one hundred grand," she went on. "You get probation, no jail time, with community service."

"Community service might present a problem," I said. "What's the get out of jail scot-free plan cost?"

"Two hundred grand," she answered. "Do you have it?"

"No, I don't," I said. "Plus I have to pay you. What will I owe you when this is done?"

"I'll take the twenty-five as if we did a plea," she said.

"Okay, I guess I'm doing community service."

"I'll talk to my friends in the probation office," she offered. "We'll find you something painless to do."

"Much appreciated," I said.

"I'll deliver the cash at lunch tomorrow," she said. "Then you get on the docket. We'll go to judge's quarters and he'll lecture you, and calm the prosecutor. You walk out a free man. Then you go straight to the probation office."

"So I'll be back on my boat in a few days?" I asked. "Hard to believe."

"Welcome to south Florida law and politics, Breeze."

"I'll have enough cash left to take you out to dinner," I said. "What do you think?"

She hadn't seen that coming. She stopped in her tracks and chewed the end of her pen. She pushed her hair back behind her ears, adjusted her glasses on her nose, and smiled at me.

"I guess I can't use ethics as an excuse not to date a client?" she said, laughing.

"I could pay you a bribe to go out with me, if you want," I said.

"I am intrigued, I admit," she said. "Let's get this business settled first, and we can talk about it later, okay?"

"Fair enough," I answered.

She gathered her things to leave, but paused at the door, studying me.

"You are not at all, who I thought you would be," she said.

"I yam what I yam," I said.

She laughed and left the room, waving backwards as the door closed behind her.

Over the next few days, Taylor brought me some dress clothes to wear to court. I listened to her instructions on how to behave in front of the judge. He was bought and paid for, but wouldn't tolerate open disrespect of the process. The prosecutor's office had been informed of the pending decision to let me off easy and they weren't happy about it. A phone call from Captain Fred magically appeased them. We were all set.

Taylor, the assistant D.A., and myself, were lead into the judge's chambers by the bailiff. Once the door was shut, the judge spoke first.

"Miss Ford, is this the defendant we discussed earlier this week?" he asked.

"Yes, your honor," she answered. "Captain Fred's close friend, Mr. Meade Breeze."

He made a check mark on a yellow legal pad, and turned to the prosecutor.

"Do you understand the nature of intervention in this case?" he asked. "And are you prepared to accept a plea of guilty, in exchange for probation and community service?"

"Yes, your honor," he replied. "The state does not wish to pursue a finding for incarceration, at this time. We reserve the right to rescind probation in the event of any future violation."

Then he turned to me.

"Mr. Breeze, do you understand the nature of that last statement?"

"I do, your honor," I said.

"It means that if you screw up, we'll reinstate the original charges, to include intent to distribute," he said firmly. "You'll serve the maximum term allowable under sentencing guidelines, if you violate the terms of your parole."

It was not a question, so I didn't comment. He then turned back to Taylor.

"Have you made the necessary arrangements with Probation and Parole?" he asked her.

"Yes, your honor," she answered. "We are to report to them directly upon the close of proceedings here today."

"I'll expect you to take personal responsibility for the defendant's compliance," he said. "Leniency was granted only through the recommendation of important people. Those people will be disappointed if we see Mr. Breeze in here again."

"I've already met with Parole," she said. "We've come up with an arrangement that should please everyone involved."

"Good," he harrumphed. "Mr. Breeze, I hope you appreciate the level of mercy that has been shown by the court. If you violate the terms of your parole, you won't appreciate the consequences."

"I won't let you down, your honor," I said humbly.

"Anything else?" he asked of all of us in general.

No one spoke. We were dismissed. I was free. Taylor grabbed me by the back of the elbow and led me at a hurried pace out of the judge's chambers, and through the courtroom. She didn't let me loose until we were out in the hallway.

"Do I celebrate now?" I asked. "That all happened so fast. It didn't seem real."

"Not here," she answered. "Keep looking humble and chastised until we get out of here. I may have bought your freedom, but I didn't buy any good will with the judge."

"He didn't have to take the bribe," I said.

"Well, yea," she said. "He kind of did. He didn't like it, but the money was enough to win him over."

"Thank God for Captain Fred," I said. "Now what?"

"We go meet your probation officer," she said.

Miranda was a long-time friend of Taylor's. She wasn't quite as attractive. Her clothes were not as trendy and expensive, but she was friendly and personable. The two of them chattered and whispered to each other like they were part of some conspiracy. I was led into Miranda's office, where I was introduced to Rob. Rob was a ranger, chief ranger at Cayo Costa State Park. I didn't understand what was going on, and the three of them left me hanging for a few seconds.

"Would someone please explain what's going on?" I asked.

Taylor was obviously proud of herself. She had used her friendships and connections to make my community service as painless as possible.

"You'll serve your community service at Cayo Costa," she beamed. "You can live on your boat. You'll be working for Rob on the island, until you log the four hundred hours required."

"I really don't have anything for you to do," said Rob. "It will be a cakewalk. Between my staff and all the volunteers, I've got too many people already."

"I'd be happy to pick up trash on the beach, or count turtle nests, or whatever," I said.

"We'll figure something out," he said. "Just come see me when you get yourself together. Miranda has given me a logbook to track your hours. She can keep an eye on you through my office."

I looked at all three of them. Each had a huge smile on their face. They barely knew me, but had gone out of their way to be nice to me. My faith in humanity was somewhat restored. I didn't deserve all this kindness.

"You three are awesome," I said. "I can't possibly thank you all enough. I'm deeply humbled, and forever in your debt."

"We all expect that you'll stay out of trouble," said Taylor. "Make sure you justify our confidence in you. These two are taking my word for it, that you're worthy of a second chance."

"I'm very appreciative," I said.

To myself, I thought about all the chances I'd already blown. How many more chances would I get? The little angel on my shoulder was telling me, that this was my wake-up call. It was time to straighten up and fly right. The little devil was nowhere to be found. I wondered about my boat. What kind of shape was *Leap of Faith* in? I wondered about Joy. Was she still hanging around somewhere? Had she waited for me? I thought about Laura, and felt guilty for lusting after Taylor. At that moment, I was overwhelmed.

"Thank you all so much," I said. "Taylor, can you take me to my boat now?"

The Marina

As we got in her car, Taylor reminded me that I had asked her out to dinner. It was the furthest thing from my mind, but as she sat behind the wheel her skirt rode up on her thighs, and I was reminded why I'd asked her out in the first place.

"You got me all dressed up, so we should go someplace nice," I said. "I assure you, this will probably be the last time you'll see me wearing dress clothes."

"You clean up nicely, Breeze," she said. "I suspect you hide some refinement under your boat bum guise."

"I used to run in different circles," I said. "But that was a long time ago, in a different world."

"That mystery man shtick is not going to work with me," she said. "Tell me all about it over a glass of champagne. My treat."

The Turtle Club was across the street from the marina. We parked near the docks, and walked to the trendy new restaurant in downtown Punta Gorda. We toasted to my freedom. She was pretty, intelligent, and very pleasant, but I was distracted. All I could think about was my boat. *Miss Leap* was just across the street. I'd been away too long. I didn't reveal my life story to her at all, instead I asked her about her job. She was more than happy to talk about herself. I learned where she grew up, where she went to school, and what she liked to do in her spare time. She learned practically nothing about me.

After we paid the tab and rose to leave, it dawned on her that I hadn't really said anything.

"How did you manage to do that?" she said. "I'm a lawyer, for God's sake. Instead of me getting information from you, you cross-examined me."

"I'm a much better listener, than I am a talker," I said. "I enjoyed listening to you."

"Well, you owe me," she said. "We'll have to do this again, so I can ask the questions."

She handed me her card as we approached her car. Under different circumstances I would have invited her aboard for a drink, but it would have to wait. I just wanted to be alone, with my boat. As a female specimen, she was pretty much perfect, but my mind was elsewhere. I needed to come to terms with my newfound legal status. I needed to know if Joy was still around somewhere. I was sure that *Leap of Faith* was a mess.

I had intended to give her a polite peck before she got in her car. As I leaned in to kiss her, she put one hand behind my head and pulled me into her. The kiss was deep and long, and very satisfying. It gave me a little chill down my spine.

"Good night, Breeze," she said. "It's been a pleasure working with you."

"Same here," I said. "Good night to you too."

"Call me," she said.

She buckled up and drove off into the night.

I walked down the gangway and onto the floating docks of Laishley Park Marina. I found *Miss Leap* in slip C-10. The shore power cord was plugged in, and her lines were secured smartly. I slid the rear door open and stepped into the salon. When I flipped on a light, I was appalled at what I saw. When I left her, she had just been riddled with bullet holes. An old nemesis had found me and tried his best to kill me. None of his bullets found me, but plenty of them had ripped through my vessel. Shattered windows were covered with plastic. The refrigerator doors were open and the power was off. It had suffered several direct hits and was obviously no longer functioning. There were dust and spider webs everywhere. Most of the holes on the port side had been patched and sanded. The starboard side holes were covered with duct tape.

Someone, probably Joy, had begun repairs. For whatever reason, they were never completed. A musty smell hung thickly in the air. I opened all the hatches to let some air in. I walked around to survey the rest of the damage. It wasn't pretty. I was facing a lot of work to make her right again. I turned on a light in my berth and saw something that touched me. There on the nightstand was a film canister. It had been wrapped in tape, and on the tape was written the name, Laura. I looked inside to see just a few sprinkles of ashes. I remembered seeing it take a direct hit during the attack. Laura's ashes had exploded all over the bunk. Did Joy recover what she could for me? If so, it was a very kind thing for her to have done. Where was she now?

I needed a beer. The tackle shop at the marina was still open. I paid eight dollars for a six-pack. I sat in my favorite spot on the aft deck, put my feet up on the transom, and tried to make sense of my life. I was free. I had paid my debts. I had enough money to live for a few years if I was frugal.

Miss Leap was badly wounded, and suffering from neglect. I had let her down. It would take an awful lot to get her to forgive me. I felt terrible about that. Joy had been here. She had taken care of my boat for a while, then left. Why? I had barely thought about Laura the whole time I was in custody. Now here she was, still in my life. I brought what was left of her outside with me. I sat her on the table and spoke, for old-time sake.

"I'm back," I said. "Never a dull moment, eh?"

She didn't answer.

The next morning, I found Oregon Rod over on A-Dock. I had asked Joy to bring my boat here, and get help from him, just before the cops took me away.

"Good God man," said Rod. "You're alive. None of us knew what happened to you."

"It's been a rough couple of months," I said. "But I need to know about Joy."

"She came in here driving your boat and asked me to take her back to Pelican Bay," he said. "The next day, she showed up in her boat. She anchored off Gilchrest Park. She was coming in here every day and working on those holes in your boat."

"What happened to her?" I asked. "Where is she?"

"One day her husband showed up here," he answered. "He started beating the shit out of her right on the dock. Me and Mark pulled him off of her. Bill from Freedom Boats called the cops. The next day she sailed out of here. I don't know where she went."

"That's not good," I said. "She ran far away from him. I can't believe he found her. I'd really like to find her, but the boat needs a lot of work first."

"I'll help you how I can, buddy," he said. "But I didn't have the money to get anything done. I've been keeping an eye on her though. Bilges are dry. Systems are okay."

"Thanks, Rod," I said. "I've got some money. I can get started right away, but I've also got this little community service thing I've gotta do."

"Whatever you need," he said.

I took him up on his offer. Over the next few weeks I used him as a second pair of hands. I got a new refrigerator and he helped me lug it onboard, and throw away the old one. I sent him off to the glass shop for new windows while I patched and sanded. I worked like a madman. Rodney was my gopher. Anytime I needed parts or supplies, he'd go fetch them. I didn't even have a car, so it was great to have his help. Each night I'd pay him in beer. He'd catch me up on the dock gossip.

Life over on A-Dock was quite the soap opera. Rodney had been dating Janie, who once dated Clete. Clete had also once dated Bonnie, but was now with Sandy. Clete had also once dated Janie. Janie and Bonnie were longtime friends. Rodney got caught kissing Bonnie, so Janie left him. It was all very hard to follow. It made me long for Pelican Bay. I learned not to leave my clothes unattended in the laundry room, so as not to displease the Laundry Nazi. I learned that everyone was welcome aboard *Emoh*, at the end of D-Dock, every night at five for happy hour. The dog on *Mojito* liked to bark. The daytime hooker on the big Viking was really a homeless women who'd found a sugar daddy. The still-homeless Terry, was allowed to plug in his Obama phone at the marina picnic tables, as long as he behaved. The old guy across from my slip looked to be a hundred years old. His dog was equally aged. It was a serious culture shock for me.

Patching bullet holes in fiberglass was tedious work. I used Marine-Tex as filler, which required a lot of sanding. The repair then had to be painted. The white pain that I used almost matched the existing paint perfectly. If you didn't look to close, you couldn't tell, but I would always know. It made me sick to think of all the pain *Miss Leap* had suffered. She wasn't herself yet. There wasn't much I could do with the interior holes. I thought about filling them with wood putty, but decided to just leave the scars. They'd always remind me to be on my toes. They'd be a unique conversation starter as well.

Finally, I reached a point where I could finish the repairs out in Pelican Bay. I hoped that once I ran her engines and cruised down Charlotte Harbor, *Miss Leap* would begin to warm up to me again.

I called Ranger Rob to let him know I was on my way. I called Miranda as well. There was nothing left to do, except to call Taylor. I'd pushed her out of my mind while I worked on the boat. I'd spent much more time worrying and wondering about Joy.

"Well, well, well," Taylor said. "Who is this stranger calling me?"
"I'm sorry," I said. "I've been working day and night to fix the boat. It's almost ready and Ranger Rob is expecting me soon."
"I'm sensing that this is a polite goodbye," she said.

"It's complicated," I said. "But, let's not do this on the phone. Can you come here? I'll explain over drinks. On me this time."

When she boarded the boat, the first thing she noticed was all the bullet scars in the teak interior. They were indeed a great conversation starter. She forgot all about the fact that I had ignored her for a month.

"I can't believe you were in here when this happened," she said. "It must have been terrifying."
"It all happened pretty fast," I said. "I didn't really have time to be afraid."

"I guess I glossed over the fact that you'd been all shot up like this," she said. "You never did tell me the whole story."

I gave her pieces of it. I had bashed a bad man in the head with a hammer, in order to stop a rape. He survived and eventually came after me. Joy and I, though not exactly a couple, were sharing our lives at the time. She had promised to wait for me. She had saved my boat, then she had disappeared. I really wanted to find her.

"I guess I'm trying to say, that even though I think you are absolutely fantastic, I have to resolve the situation with Joy. She may be out there somewhere, still waiting for me. When you kissed me, it gave me chills. You're smart and sexy and I desire you, but I have to honor what Joy and I had, and what she did for me. I hope you understand."

"Wow," she said. "A dope dealing, boat bum with relationship ethics. I can't figure you out, but yes, I understand. Go do what you have to do. Just don't screw up your probation."

"Thanks, Taylor," I said. "You're the best. Who knows what the future holds for me, but I'm grateful to you, for everything."

"You keep my number," she said. "You never know when you'll need a good lawyer."

"Or a dinner date," I replied.

We clinked our glasses together, finished our drinks, and parted ways.

Cayo Costa

As I guided *Leap of Faith* down Charlotte Harbor, my thoughts turned to home. It felt like it had been years since I'd seen the peaceful waters of Pelican Bay, or walked the white beaches of Cayo Costa, even though I'd only been gone a few months. So much had happened since the day Enrique had ripped apart my world with automatic weapons fire.

He was in jail now, along with the rest of Bald Mark's men. Bald Mark himself had been taken into custody, but had posted bail and somehow delayed his trial indefinitely. As I had recently learned, money and influence worked wonders in the south Florida legal system. I felt confident that he wouldn't make a move against me, with all the publicity surrounding the arrest of him and his cartel members in the Keys.

It was a leisurely three hour boat ride from Punta Gorda to the coast, at seven knots. When the entrance to Pelican Bay came into view, I used binoculars to look for Joy's boat, *Another Adventure*. I would easily recognize it if it was there, but no such luck. I felt a twinge of disappointment. Slowing to four knots, we crawled past the boats already at anchor until we reached our familiar spot near the southern terminus of the bay. I set the anchor firmly and let the engine idle for a few minutes. When I shut it down, I said "*Good Job, Miss Leap.*" She was in a better mood now that we were home, but our relationship still wasn't a hundred percent restored.

It was late in the afternoon, not quite happy hour. The ranger station would still be open until five, so I went in to see if Rob was available. He greeted me with a friendly smile and a firm handshake.

"Welcome to Cayo Costa, Breeze," he said.

"It's great to be here," I replied. "Have you figured out what to do with me?"

"I've given it some thought," he answered. "Here's the plan. The workboat arrives with the volunteers at eight in the morning. Once you see them dock, come on in. Your job will be to police the beaches for litter and such. I'll give you a four-wheeler, gloves, trash bags, whatever you need."

"Hell, Rob," I said. "The island is only seven miles long. With a four wheeler I can do the whole beach in one day."

"What I thought you could do," he countered, "Was to drive to a spot, then walk and cover a mile or so on foot. Different spot each day. Just a leisurely walk on the beach. You'll be looking for beer cans, dead animals, whatever."

"Sounds like easy duty," I admitted. "I've walked these beaches, and it's rare to see any trash."

"Just put in a few hours, Monday through Friday," he said. "We'll mark you down for eight hours in the log. Your weekends are free. In ten weeks it will all be over with. Community service completed."

"I really thought this would be harder," I said. "Thanks."

"I don't want to have to babysit a grown man, Breeze," he said. "Just show up, stay low, and I'll vouch for you with the probation office. It's all good."

"You've got a deal," I said. "Tomorrow at eight?"

"After the workboat arrives," he answered. "See you then."

By the time I returned to the boat, it was happy hour. I grabbed a beer and sat down to consider my good fortune. I had never wanted to face my past. I'd been running from it for years. I'd taken some strange pleasure in sticking it to The Man. Living as an outlier and a pirate had become a large part of my identity. Making things right with the law had been thrust upon me. It hadn't been my choice, but here I was. I had ten weeks of beachcombing and one year of probation in front of me. After that, I'd be completely legitimate. I could reapply for a new passport and travel. I could get a real job if necessary. I'd have to support myself in the future somehow, but for now I was in pretty good shape. I had about sixty grand in cash, with zero bills to pay. I could make that last a long time.

Where was Joy? She didn't have a phone and neither did I. She might show up here looking for me at some point, but I couldn't count on that. I decided to use my weekends looking for her. The fact that *Another Adventure* had a six foot draft, severely limited her options in these waters. She didn't like the Keys, so I figure she had to be hiding on the west coast of Florida somewhere. Somewhere her husband couldn't find her.

I popped another beer and made a mental checklist of the places she might hide. To the south, there were no secluded spots away from people other than the backwaters of Fort Myers Beach. Going to shore would be risky if her husband was still looking for her though. Below that, was Naples, Marco and the Ten Thousand Islands. Goodland was the only good hole, but I doubted she could get her boat in there. To the north, Chadwick Cove at Englewood Beach was a possibility. She'd fit in with the locals there and there was plenty of water. Sarasota was too public. Longboat Key or Bradenton were possibilities. She could hide up in the Manatee River and never be found, but she'd have to get provisions somewhere. Any further north than that and she'd have to rely on blending in with the hundreds of other boats in someplace like St. Petersburg or Clearwater. I wasn't familiar with those areas. The list was getting pretty long.

I started to relax while drinking beer number three. I really had been lucky to stay out of jail. The various agencies, lawyers and one judge had taken almost all of my money, but it was worth it to be free. I could stop being paranoid every minute of every day. Bald Mark was the only remaining wildcard. I hoped his energies were devoted to staying out of jail himself.

I spent the next five days reporting for duty as chief beach cleaner. I spent a few hours in the morning looking for trash or debris. After checking back in with the ranger's office, I had my afternoons free. I used them to work on the boat. Endless patching and sanding was my penance for allowing such damage to *Miss Leap*. If that dumbass Enrique had been smart, he'd have put a bunch of holes below the waterline. My boat wouldn't be here to patch.

I made myself work in the afternoon sun, no matter how hot it was. My sweat was mixed with fiberglass and sanding dust. I talked to my boat as I worked. I tried to soothe her. I promised not to let anything like that happen to her again. We were making progress. Each day I worked right up until happy hour. I'd jump overboard to cool off, rinse with fresh water, and grab that first cold beer. The labor kept my mind from wandering and provided me with a sense of self-discipline. I'd become a lazy son of a bitch over the past few years. Living on a boat in the islands will do that to a person.

Saturday arrived and I set out early for Fort Myers Beach. Other than the wakes from all the pleasure boaters, it was a glorious trip. I loved this stretch of the waterway. *Miss Leap* hummed and purred the whole way. She was finally getting over her anger with me. We were going to be okay. We passed under the Matanzas Bridge at noon. I went straight for the backwater where I had friends. They were friends with Joy too, or had been when she was around.

One-legged Beth arrived in her skiff as soon as we were settled on the anchor. She tied off and hopped aboard like a gymnast. We exchanged hugs and greetings.

"If you're looking for Joy," she began. "She was here about a month ago. She only stayed a day. She loaded up with groceries and split. She did the same thing a month before that."

"Where does she go?" I asked.

"She wouldn't tell us," Beth answered. "Told us not to tell she was ever here if anyone came asking."

"If she comes back again," I said. "Tell her I'm in Pelican Bay for at least the next nine weeks."

"She looked all busted up the first time she was here," she said.

"Her husband found her in Punta Gorda," I told her. "She was trying to take care of my boat, and it got her in trouble. She's hiding from him."

"That explains a lot," she said. "She had Robin escort her to the store. I thought it was because of those bums that hang out back there. I offered to go with her, but she said she needed a man along."

"Just tell her where I'll be if you see her again," I said. "Tell her I need to see her. Tell her I'll wait for her."

"She'll be back," she said. "She'll be thrilled you're looking for her. A woman knows these things."

"Thanks, Beth," I said. "Bring the guys over later for drinks. It's good to see you."

She hoped back into her skiff like a monkey and drove off towards Diver Dan's boat. This place hadn't changed. The same boats were in the same places. It was good to be able to rely on some things staying the same.

That night the three amigos joined me for happy hour. Diver Dan brought a bottle of cheap rum. One-legged Beth drank beer. Robin drank instant coffee mixed with Carnation instant breakfast. They were still cleaning boat bottoms and picking up odd-jobs here and there. Beth's boat still had no motor. Dan's white beard was fuller and thicker. They were an unlikely trio, but I enjoyed their company. I told them all about my dalliance with the legal system. They all agreed that I had a special knack for going through large sums of money in record time. These folks were collecting food stamps and going to the food bank once a week so they could eat. I'd burned through a couple of million bucks in a few short years. We shared a most unlikely friendship.

I chuckled at myself and my predicaments. One day I was having a fancy dinner and champagne with a talented lawyer lady in a tailored suit. The next day I was drinking cheap beer with a toothless, braless, one-legged woman and her two boyfriends. Such was the life of Breeze.

The next day I ran the gauntlet of homeless dudes that hung out behind the supermarket. I could see why a woman wouldn't want to do it alone. The Mangrove Mob numbered three vagrants. I think they had four teeth between them. They were so dirty from sleeping on the ground, I expected to see Spanish moss hanging off their limbs. They didn't bother with me though. I got my groceries and split.

Back in Pelican Bay I returned to my routine. Ranger Rob sent me off to the beach each morning. I tended to the boat each afternoon. I'd finished filling all the bullet holes. I kept fairing and sanding until I had them all as smooth as they could get. The paint was giving me fits, so I re-sanded what I had painted and tried again. I couldn't quite get it perfect, but it was as good as it was going to get without repainting the whole boat.

Over beers I'd scan my charts, looking for a place where Joy might hide. I worked on the assumption that she was within a day's journey from Fort Myers Beach. I made marks on the chart sixty miles to the south, north and west. To the south she could be somewhere in the Ten Thousand Islands. Her deep draft limited her, but there were still dozens of possible anchorages. She'd never be found down there, probably not even by me. To the north, my mark was just above Englewood Beach. She'd have to pass right by Pelican Bay to get to Fort Myers Beach, so I ruled that out. She'd stop in if she was passing by. To the west was the Caloosahatchee River. Labelle was a possibility. It had a free city dock, but it didn't have a grocery store. She would need to leave for food.

I decided she had to be hiding south of Marco Island, somewhere amongst the mangroves and mire of the Ten Thousand Islands. It's a beautiful, but desolate area. Mosquitoes are a real problem. It's an extension of the Everglades really, except fed by saltwater instead of fresh. I noted half a dozen likely places she could be, that would accept her six foot draft. It would take me a full day to get there. I'd only have time to look in two or three spots in one weekend.

Then I worried that if something went wrong with the boat, or the weather turned bad, I wouldn't make it back by Monday morning. Under no circumstances could I screw up my community service and probation. I was starting to come to terms with my new position in life. I was making things right. I was becoming a legal citizen, not an outlaw. I could walk around freely without looking over my shoulder. It lifted a huge burden off my shoulders. It cleared my mind and allowed me to enjoy life. The only thing missing was Joy.

So what about her? We had not been in a committed relationship. We were friends who occasionally had sex. We were kindred souls, living on boats, hiding from the mainstream of society and doing a good job of it. I could brush it off, make a call to Taylor, and move on. The problem there was Joy's promise to wait for me. It wasn't like her to make a promise like that. It felt sincere when she said it. I decided to stay put. She'd go back to Fort Myers Beach, Beth would tell her I was here, and it would be up to her after that.

It was the right decision. Two weeks later I saw *Another Adventure*, under full sail, breezing into the unmarked entrance channel of my little bay. The sight of her boat caused my heart to flutter. I hopped into my dinghy and set off at top speed to intercept her. Instead of pulling alongside, I ran fast circles around her, whooping and hollering like a wild west Indian.

"Breezy boy, you fool," she screamed over the whine of my little Mercury outboard. "Get up here and let me look at you."

"Oh Joy, oh Joy," I sang. "Welcome back. I miss your grit and all your sass. When I get on board, I will grab your ass."

She laughed and started bringing down her sails. I hovered off her stern as the boat slowed and she went forward to drop anchor. When she was settled on the hook, I started to approach. Before I could tie off, she ran across the deck and dove overboard. I pulled her up into the dinghy and she dove on top of me, covering me with salty kisses.

"You are a sight for sore eyes, Breeze," she said. "I didn't know if I'd ever see you again."

"You had me worried as well," I said. "I heard about what happened in Punta Gorda."

"He's lost his mind, Breeze," she said. "There was evil in his eyes. He would have killed me. It really scared me. I don't want to ever face him again. I thought I'd lost him for good down here."

"Let's worry about that later," I said. "Are you okay?"

"I was hurt pretty bad," she answered. "My face was all black and blue and I'm pretty sure I had broken ribs. They still hurt. I've been laid up recovering."

"Where?" I asked.

"A place called Sugar Bay," she answered. "Just south and east of Goodland."

It was not one of the possible places I had guessed at. I knew Sugar Bay. There was a hump at the entrance with only five foot depths.

"How the hell did you get in there?" I asked.

"I'd sit out at Coon Key and wait for a big high tide," she answered. "Sometimes it might be in the middle of the night. I bumped bottom every time."

"Good place to hide," I said. "I wouldn't have found you."

"The bugs were pretty wicked at night," she said. "And I'm out of money. I haven't been able to beg, borrow or steal a dime, since I left Punta Gorda. I'm flat out busted. I'm sorry, Breeze."

"I've got a little stash left," I said. "It isn't much, but we'll survive for a while."

"I hate being a dependent," she said. "I made myself some promises when I ran away from my husband. But I don't have much of a choice at this point."

I explained my community service deal to her. I couldn't leave until that was complete. I made the simple calculation that what money I had left, would last half as long supporting two people, and two boats. Eventually, we'd have to generate some income. For now, I was just happy to be with her again.

I took her back to *Leap of Faith*. She didn't mention the bullet holes, or the repairs. She simply shed her wet clothes on the aft deck and stepped inside naked. She unbuttoned my shirt, dropped my shorts and pushed me onto the settee. Always before, when we had sex, it was playful and casual. This time it was loving and soft. She held me tight like I might get away if she let go. It was sweet. She laid her head on my chest afterwards, listening to my heartbeat. She started to cry.

"He hurt me bad, Breeze," she said. "Don't let him hurt me again."

"You're safe now," I said. "You're safe with me."

She continued sobbing for a long time. No amount of stroking or gentle words could make it stop. The violent encounter with her husband had changed her, broken her spirit. She was counting on me to protect her, and support her. Just like that, once again I was responsible for another human life. I didn't know what to think about that.

Joy and Breeze

Joy wasn't her real name. A few years back she had drugged her abusive husband, drained the bank account, and ran away. She chose a new name, bought an old sailboat, and made a new life. She cut off all of her hair, hid out in the Keys for a while, and made her way north to Fort Myers Beach, where we had met. She had been completely carefree, loose and happy prior to my arrest.

She wasn't the prettiest woman I'd ever been with. She was short and slightly stocky. She wore that butch haircut that I didn't like, but her face was cute enough to pull it off. Her main physical attribute was a perfect ass. Her ass was like the swinging watch of a hypnotist. It put men in a trance.

Although we had been sharing a life together, she had held me at arm's length emotionally. Sex was for fun. We never mentioned commitment. We were playful with each other, but we never uttered the "L" word. We lived for today and today only, which suited me just fine.

Now she was different. For the first week, she stayed with me constantly aboard *Leap of Faith*. We snuggled a lot, held hands as we walked the beach. She looked deep into my eyes often, studying me. Sex turned into lovemaking. She wasn't her former vivacious, flirty self. She was attentive and gentle. Her infinite confidence and ego had been shattered. She was leaning on me, trying to hold on.

During the second week, she started spending a little more time on her own boat, usually while I was patrolling the beach for beer cans. She relaxed somewhat, but I'd notice her looking around, checking out new boats coming in. I finally asked her what she was afraid of.

"Joy, you know that no one can find you here, except by boat," I said. "What are you afraid of?"

"He has a boat," she said. "The son of a bitch has a boat."

This was new information, which had a negative connotation. I learned much more about her torturous husband that day. She called him Jerk-Off Joe. As the sexual torture progressed, he stopped having sex with his victim. Instead he pleasured himself as he inflicted pain on her. He got off on the torture, not the woman.

His boat was a big Carver motor yacht. No one knew about it, not even his parents. He formed a shell company, which leased it to another shell company. It was his bug-out vehicle, in case of the zombie apocalypse, economic collapse, or world war. He kept it stocked with freeze-dried food, canned goods, and lots of water. It was in a marina in Galveston, about an hour from their home in a Houston suburb. It rarely left the slip. It was named *Fifty Shades*. He ran the motors occasionally and kept it in good repair, but he really wasn't a yachtsman. She thought he was afraid to pilot the thing. Would he have the nerve to bring it to Florida in search of her?

I asked about weapons. She said he had a handgun, but never fired it. I asked about money. She said he had plenty, and liked to spend it. It would take a long time to get to Florida from Texas, but it had been almost three months since her encounter with him. My vacation from eternal vigilance was short-lived. No one was looking for me anymore. Someone might be looking for Joy.

We discussed various plans of action over the next week or so. We decided that once I finished my community service, we'd go on the move. We'd have to make some money eventually, and there was no way to do that on Cayo Costa. I asked how she financed her lifestyle in Fort Myers Beach.

"Slipping Mickeys," she said. "Roofies, sleepy drops."

"You're kidding me," I said.

"Nope. I worked the hotel bars, I zeroed in on the guys looking to cheat on their wives. I let them buy me a couple rounds. I doped up their drink. Before they got totally zonked I'd help them back to their room. Once they passed out, I took whatever cash they had in their wallet."

"And you made a living like that?" I asked.

"I don't need much. I've got no bills," she answered. "Sometimes I'd get a few hundred bucks. Sometimes I'd only get forty or fifty. A few times I struck out. People don't carry cash like they used to. I never took credit cards or jewelry, too risky. If I hit the Holiday Inn one night, I wouldn't go back there for a couple weeks. I spread it around the island, couple times a week."

"We could do better on the east coast," I said. "There's more money, more hotels, more marinas. We need to figure out a way to tweak the scam though. We'll need more than a few hundred bucks a week if we want to stay on the move. We'll have to decide on which boat to take, and what to do with the other boat. I'd have to pull my weight as well. Lots to figure out."

"You're really willing to go back to being an outlaw, for me?" she asked.

"Stick with what you're good at, Dad always said."

I finished out my duty on the beach with Ranger Rob. We made both boats ready to go and said our farewells. Rob let me use his phone to call Miranda to check off the first phase of my probation. So far so good. My only remaining restriction was that I couldn't leave the state of Florida until my one year term was complete.

Joy had her sails up and raised anchor while I let my diesel warm up. I was faster motoring, but she could keep up easily in a decent wind. In the long straightaway off Captiva Island, she had a nice point of sail and passed me. When we turned at the bend of Sanibel, she lost her advantage and I retook the lead. I turned off the ICW to go under the Sanibel Causeway, while she continued on to clear the taller bridge at Punta Rassa. I anchored in the river with the other misfits and waited for her arrival, about forty-five minutes later.

We spent a few days planning and visiting with the three backwater amigos of Fort Myers Beach. One-legged Beth, Diver Dan, and sidekick Robin, were sorry to hear that we'd be moving on. We actually were pretty weak on strategy. We'd head to the east coast, poke around and see what came up as far as scams or opportunities. I was struggling to take greater advantage of Joy's barroom abilities to charm older men. I had an idea how I could bilk tourists, but wasn't sure how profitable it might be.

We decided that *Leap of Faith* would be our vessel of choice. The mast height of *Another Adventure*, combined with its six foot draft, made it a liability. It couldn't go under a lot of the bridges and we'd have a tough time anchoring. We left Joy's boat under the watchful eye of Beth, promising to return someday. Joy wouldn't think of putting it up for sale. It had been her escape from a life of horror. She loved her old boat as much as I loved mine. I liked that about her. I secretly figured that she needed it as an insurance policy, in case things didn't work out between us.

We still hadn't made any official commitment to each other, but here we were, joined at the hip in search of adventure. I was running from her past now, instead of my own. We were about to become the maritime version of Bonnie and Clyde. The little devil on my shoulder thought it was great. *Loot and plunder!* The little angel on my other shoulder just shook its head in disgust. I knew better, but I was doing it anyway. Choosing to do the wrong thing was getting easier, I noticed. As I further contemplated this new crossroad I'd come to, I had the strong intuition that things would end badly. There was a dark cloud on the horizon, and we were sailing right into it.

I shook off that foreboding feeling as we left the coast and headed inland across the Okochobee Waterway. It was nice to have another set of hands when we passed through the locks. Joy was happy to be on the move. There was no way we'd run into Jerk-Off Joe in these waters. The cities of Florida's east coast were a congested mess of overdevelopment. The odds of bumping into him over there seemed slim. We relaxed and worked on refining our plan.

Joy explained how she targeted married men. The easiest sign was the pale band around the finger where a wedding ring normally was worn. She didn't feel bad about stealing from a cheater. Failing the missing ring, she simply asked them. She said she could just tell if they lied. Should could walk into a bar, study all the men, and guess who was married and who was not. She claimed a ninety percent success rate.

I had a vague notion of selling fake charter fishing trips. Almost every marina in Florida has a row of fishing boats, with signs and pictures of fish caught. They didn't fish every day. There were always a number of boats sitting idle in charter boat row. I'd hang out, walking the docks. I'd identify tourists and approach them about a fishing trip. I'd claim to be the mate on one of the boats still in its slip. I'd talk them into a charter, and ask for a deposit to hold their spot on Thursday, or whatever day. I'd insist on cash. The captain would be surprised when they showed up to go fishing. I'd be long gone.

I pressed Joy to see how far she would go to maximize her take from the men in the hotel bars. I gathered that she was game for most anything, short of actually sleeping with the dude. I decided on blackmail. Before she drugged him, she'd find out his wife's name. After she drugged him, she'd verify that name on his phone. She would undress him, unlock the door to let me in, and I'd take pictures of the two of them in compromising positions. I'd leave with the phone. When he woke up, she'd demand a thousand dollars not to send the photos to his wife. She'd be dressed, sober, and armed. I'd be in the hotel lounge. When he returned with the cash, I'd give him the phone.

We went over various scenarios, figuring out what might go wrong. We'd hit one man, in one hotel bar, and move on. During the day I'd walk the docks. At night we'd unleash Joy on some unsuspecting businessman from Toledo. We'd carefully select our targets to exclude men who might get physical. We'd focus on the middle-aged, pot-bellied desk jockeys. We'd avoid the wealthy yachtsmen and jet-setters. We'd stay on the move. We'd never mention *Leap of Faith*, or our real names. We'd give thousand dollar lessons to a trail of chastened husbands from Stuart to Miami. We'd disappoint dozens of potential fishermen from West Palm Beach to St. Augustine. We'd stash the cash and retire to the west coast to live in peace, until the money ran out.

Partners in *Crime*

Our trip across the state was uneventful. We left the St. Lucie River, and took a mooring ball at Sunset Bay Marina and Anchorage, near Stuart. We spent the afternoon getting a feel for our surroundings. Using the dinghy, we were able to locate an assortment of charter boat docks in Stuart and nearby Manatee Pocket. We scoped out the waterfront bars, concentrating on those within close proximity to hotels. We stopped for an early dinner at Finz Waterfront Grille.

We eliminated most of the waterfront hotels after our tour. They were smaller, boutique establishments catering mostly to fishermen of the upper crust variety. We were more likely to find our desired prey a few blocks inland. Small time businessmen tended to favor the chains, like Days Inn, or Hampden Inn. Finally, we hit on a Marriot with a busy bar.

We came back after nine that night. There was music, clinking of cutlery and tinkling of ice in high-ball glasses. Joy moved about taking stock of the men in attendance. I sat in the corner of the bar, trying not to watch her too closely. She wore a clinging dress, with thin straps, that hugged her round ass just right. Men approached her frequently, but they were all the wrong type. The majority of these guys were fairly young, and fit. There wasn't an out of shape loser among them. After an hour she gave me a shrug from across the room. I nodded and left the bar. We met down the street, two blocks away.

"That was a waste of time," she said. "Completely wrong crowd."

"Don't sweat it," I replied. "Look around some more tomorrow while I hit the docks. We'll find the right situation somewhere in this town."

I struck out in my attempt to sell fake fishing trips the next day. We were off to a less than stellar start as a con team. At least I learned a few things. The fancy marinas with multi-million dollar sport fishing yachts, kept a close eye on all activity on the dock. They also had video surveillance. I found the smaller, less expensive marinas more to my liking. I made mental notes of the layout of two of them in Manatee Pocket.

When I met back up with Joy, she seemed enthusiastic. She had found a couple bars that weren't inside of hotels, but directly next door. She said she could just smell the desperation on the men who drank there. She felt confident that she could find her patsy there that night.

She picked him out of the crowd like a lioness culls the weakest water buffalo. He was a bit uptight at first. The booze served to loosen him up, as Joy poured on the charm. He thought she was a hooker. She didn't flinch. She just rolled with it.

"I'm not normally a call girl, honey," she told him. "But for the right price you can call me anything you want."

"What's the right price, darling?" he asked.

"I can make your night for five hundred," she answered. "But I can make your whole life for a grand. Cash only."

He took a huge slug of his drink. Some of it dribbled down his chin as he slid his barstool back. He was shaking his head yes, as he tried to swallow the booze. He pointed to the ATM in the lobby and walked towards it. It was the perfect opportunity for her to spike the remainder of his drink. I watched her in admiration. She was a pro at this. She waved at the bartender and asked for another round. When our target returned, he was eager to get the party started. The bartender placed another drink in front of his unfinished one.

"I'd rather skip right to the business at hand," he said to Joy.

"Drink up, lover boy," she said. "I'm gonna need another, to help loosen my inhibitions, if you know what I mean."

He accepted this reasoning, and finished the spiked drink. She took his empty and slid the new one in front of him. Before he could finish it, he began to appear groggy. Joy got his room key before he was totally incoherent. Next, she was helping him to the elevator.

"Poor fellow can't hold his liquor," she said, to no one in particular. I followed and jumped into the elevator at the last second. He couldn't make it to the room. I threw one of his arms over my shoulder, and humped him down the hall to his door. Joy opened it with his key, and I dumped him on the bed.

We won't need to take pictures," she said. "He's got a thousand bucks in cash in his wallet."

"Good," I said. "I really didn't need to see this joker naked."

We pocketed his cash and vanished into the night, taking a side hallway to a little used exit. We split up and met at the dinghy. Back onboard we celebrated her success over cold beers. The next afternoon I took a two hundred dollar deposit from a Midwestern family for a fishing trip that would never happen. We celebrated my success in the same fashion. We'd acquired twelve hundred dollars in two days. It was time to move on.

We traveled just a few miles north, and found a spot to anchor near the Jensen Beach Causeway. Conchy Joe's Seafood Restaurant had a dinghy dock, so we landed there for dinner.

"So what do you think, Breezy Boy?" she asked. "Can you live like this? Moving from town to town scamming folks for a living?"

"For a while," I answered. "We save up enough to quit. Take our retirement a little bit at a time. Let the heat die down."

"Come back with our hair dyed and start all over again?" she asked.

"If necessary, but there are a million bars on this coast," I said. "We never hit the same place twice. We stay with the tourists. Don't let the locals get a read on us."

"That was my mistake in Fort Myers Beach," she said. "I hung out too much with the locals. Bartenders all knew me. I wore out my welcome."

"Won't be a problem over here," I assured her. "We get in, we get out, we move on."

That's how it went for the next several months. Joy took another grand from an unsuspecting conventioneer at the Hutchinson Island Resort. He had more tolerance to the drug than our previous victim. We had to play out the whole blackmail scam. Joy undressed him and laid him back on the pillows. She unlocked the door and handed me his phone. She straddled him, and sat down on his waist. I snapped some photos. I made sure not to show her face, but there was no doubt that a naked woman was sitting on top of someone's husband. Then she positioned her head over his crotch for another picture. His eyes were closed, but he looked to be in a state of ecstasy.

We had to slap him around to wake him up. Joy had gotten his wife's name earlier. I had the phone poised to send the incriminating photos to her. When he figured out what was going on, he pled for mercy. He'd do anything, just don't send those pictures.

"A thousand bucks," said Joy. "You can buy your phone back for a thousand bucks."

"No problem," he said. "Please, don't ruin me."

"Get the money," I chimed in. "We'll wait in the lobby. You get the phone when we get the cash. Don't leave the hotel. Don't signal for help. I'll be watching you. He did as he was told, and we snuck off into the night like the thieves that we were. It would be a long time before he tried to pick up a strange woman in a hotel bar.

The next morning I collected my bogus deposit from four college kids who wanted to go sail fishing. I walked out of the Nettles Island Marina with two crisp hundred dollar bills, and took the dinghy back to *Leap of Faith*. We immediately pulled up anchor and continued north. We anchored just to the south of green daybeacon "9" off Causeway Island, in the entrance to Faber Cover, near Fort Pierce. We took the dinghy into Harbortown Marina, and ran our scams from there.

Next, we anchored in the Vero Beach Basin and found a sucker at the Loggerhead Club. I failed on the docks. I failed again at Indian River. I tried the Sebastian River Marina, Capt'n Butchers, Fins, and Capt Hiram's Marina. Tourist traffic on the docks was slow. The few tourist groups I tried, were not impressed with my pitch, or were suspicious. Joy was having no such problems. She was bringing in all the revenue, pulling all the weight.

Instead of brooding over this, I decided to enlist her in my efforts. She started accompanying me to the fishing fleets, wearing really short shorts and a bikini top. Suddenly everyone wanted to go fishing. We executed successful hit and run missions all way up the east coast of Florida. We cruised from Melbourne, to Cocoa, Cape Canaveral, Titusville, New Smyrna Beach, to Port Orange. We spent two weeks in Daytona. It was there that we ran into trouble.

We had turned east off the waterway just south of the Memorial Bridge, and dropped the hook in a cozy anchorage near a yacht club. Over the first week we visited what felt like hundreds of hotels and bars all along the beach. Things were going along just fine, until we hit a dry spell. Three nights in a row we failed to find a suitable target. The crowds were so diverse, Joy said she couldn't get a good vibe. College kids rubbed elbows with senior citizens, surfers, tourists and body builders.

She lost her patience, and focus, on the fourth night of our losing streak. She selected a man who I thought was too young, too fit, and clearly not in our choice demographic group. I shook my head no from across the bar, but she ignored me. I watched them exchange pleasantries and sit down for a drink. She was so quick and smooth when she spiked his beverage, I hardly saw it. Thirty minutes later he started to nod off at the bar.

I made my way to the elevator just in time to help Joy get the guy loaded inside. In his room, she undressed him and I fiddled with his phone trying to find the camera function. As she mounted him, he flipped her over on the bed and pinned her down. Even drugged, he was too strong for her. He spoke, but his speech was too slurred to understand. As he hovered over her, slobber dribbled down his chin and onto her bare breasts. If that wasn't disgusting enough, he started trying to hump her like a puppy on a pillow. Joy screamed.

I grabbed him from behind and shoved him to the floor. Joy jumped up and started to dress. His wallet was on the nightstand directly next to him. He was still awake, but incoherent. As I snatched up his wallet he managed a feeble kick in the direction of my groin. As I backed away he managed to trip me with a foot. I tossed the wallet to Joy from where I lay.

"Get your gun from your purse," I yelled.

"Shit, Breeze," she yelled back. "This is going to hell quick."

I crawled a few yards to give myself some space. As I got to my feet, I saw Joy, in her bra and panties, pointing the gun at our not so helpless victim. I found four hundred bucks in his wallet. I put it in my pocket and tossed the wallet on the bed. I took the gun from Joy and held it on him as she finished dressing. He was still on the floor, leaning against the dresser, and trying to figure out what was going on. We'd botched up this job something awful. He got a good long look at me, we got only a portion of our usual money, and trouble was in the air.

"Go now," I instructed Joy. "Hurry back to the dinghy. I'll meet you there shortly."

"Come with me," she said. "Hurry up."

"We go separate," I said. "I'll go along the beach. You take the main drag and don't stop."

I held the gun on him until she was gone. He just sat there with a curious look on his face. I was pretty sure he said "what the fuck?" I tucked the gun in my shorts and made my exit. As usual, I took a side hall to a side exit door and snuck out into the night. I crossed over to the beach and walked purposely towards our meeting spot. When I got to the dinghy, Joy had the motor running.

"Let's roll," I said. "We're pulling up anchor tonight."

"You're going to travel the ICW at night?" she asked.

"I just want to move the boat in case anyone recognizes us," I answered.

"I'm sorry, Breeze," she said. "I fucked up."

"Yes, you did," I replied. "But this ain't the time to bicker about it."

I got the anchor up and Joy steered us north in the dark. I took over and kept us in the middle of the channel. We took turns looking at the chart, trying to find a place to anchor again for the rest of the night. Nothing looked right from the water at night. There were lights everywhere. It was hard to see. We ended up traveling north for three hours until we came to the Flagler Beach Bridge. We squeezed into a side channel that led to an abandoned cement factory. Once I got the boat settled, I went and found Joy. She was brooding in the salon.

"What the hell was that all about?" I asked.

"I got antsy," she said. "He was so eager I thought it would be easy."

"You should have known better," I responded. "He was too fit, not in our target group."

"You can stop busting my chops," she said. "I know I screwed up."

"If he had clobbered me," I started again. "You'd be his bitch right about now. I could have woken up to watch him screwing you, and you'd have deserved it. This is a dangerous game we're playing. We've got to keep the odds in our favor at all times, or take a pass."

She threw a book at my head. I dodged it, but it was close. "You didn't have to be so damned graphic," she screamed at me. "I told you I messed up. I'm sorry, okay? I could use a little compassion instead of condemnation."

"It would have broken my heart if he had gotten to you, Joy," I said softly. "It made me sick to see him on top of you."

She came to me and we embraced softly. We held each other for a few minutes. Finally, she looked up at me with a new sparkle in her eyes.

"We'll both feel better with you on top of me," she said. "Come on. Let's leave this nastiness behind us.

She led me to bed and soon all was forgotten.

Second Thoughts

In the morning, I woke early. I let Joy sleep and took my coffee out on the back deck. In the early light, I could see the Sea Ray factory on shore. It was already bustling with activity. I took the opportunity to reconsider what we'd been doing. I hadn't really had a chance to reflect. We'd been living in the moment, hopping from town to town, cruising the bars to make our scores. Joy was doing all the work, and taking most of the risks. Until last night neither of us had given it a second thought. Riding the high seas in search of adventure had made me feel strong and proud. Sneaking around hotel bars made me feel like a petty thief.

I was doing it for Joy, sure, but really I was doing it just to be with Joy. If it had been up to me, we'd have stayed in Pelican Bay, growing dope. If her husband found us there, we'd have dealt with him. She felt the need to run, and I completely understood that. I'd been running for years. So there we were, a pair of outlaws, living on the outskirts of society. We were making our way on stealth and wits. We were off the grid, surviving on the spoils of our scams. I didn't feel good about it. Something was eating at me. We'd run into real trouble, sooner or later.

As the sun rose over the Atlantic Ocean, my thoughts turned to Laura. She'd been dead a long time now, and I thought of her less and less as the time passed. That thought saddened me. I almost never spoke to her ashes anymore, what little was left of them. I'd become too busy to commune with her memory. Sitting quietly in Pelican Bay, I could feel her presence. Now, I was moving constantly. I had Joy in my daily life. Big city lights and the east coast tourist paradise kept me distracted. I decided I couldn't live like this much longer.

When Joy woke up, we talked about it over breakfast. We decided to count up our money, lay out a plan to hit a few more towns, and retire when we reached a monetary goal. After that, we'd wing it. At mid-day, we pulled up anchor and continued north once again.

We made our way up the Palm Coast to St. Augustine. There, we profited off a convention being held at a golf resort. We anchored in the Pine Island anchorage near Jacksonville Beach.

I sold a few fake fishing trips out of the Palm Cove Marina. We suckered a few conventioneers at the local Ramada Inn.

At this point, I didn't see any reason to continue heading north. Fernandina Beach was a long way, with little of interest for us in between. We turned south and skipped over all the towns we'd already visited. Below Stuart we started up operations again. Jupiter and Palm Beach were full of extremely wealthy types, yachties, Tiger Woods, and Donald Trump had homes there. We anchored near North Palm Beach and took a cab into West Palm. We had dinner at McCormick and Schmidts. As we walked the outdoor mall in the downtown area, we saw mostly elderly couples. They were smartly dressed for a night on the town. We checked a few bars, but nothing felt right. It wasn't our kind of town.

We had better luck in Riviera Beach. After that we anchored in Lake Worth. We were able to set up camp and make nightly raids into the surrounding neighborhoods. From there we continued south to Lantana, Boynton Beach, Delray, and Boca Raton. This stretch of the waterway was a treasure trove of older single men who were highly susceptible to Joy's charms. Most of them gladly offered to pay for an hour alone with her. They'd pop a Viagra while Joy spiked their drink. We put them to sleep gently and took their cash. Joy always covered their old man erections with a sheet before we left the room. I'd go to bed and dream about pup tents.

The money was piling up and I was ready to call it quits. Joy was not. We argued a little, but I didn't have the heart to stand up to her. She'd battled back from her depression and sense of helplessness after her husband roughed her up way back in Punta Gorda. She had regained her independent streak. I didn't want to spoil that for her.

We raided Deerfield Beach and Pompano Beach. We moved around to an assortment of anchorages near Fort Lauderdale. The hunting was particularly good there. We stayed a little too long and got recognized by some fellow travelers. We snuck away at dawn the next morning bound for Miami. I insisted that this would be our last stop. Any further south was too close to old dangers for me. Biscayne Bay was all that separated us from the Keys, and my old nemesis, Bald Mark.

I hated Miami, but it too, was full of likely targets for Joy's act. We worked the Art Deco District, with its numerous hotels and fancy restaurants, and the trendy South Beach area. It was Hollywood East, with lots of plastic boobs, cocaine cowboys, and lonely old men. Money rained down on Joy. It was so easy for her, be nice to the gentlemen, put him to sleep, and take his money. The old codgers here still carried a lot of cash. She didn't flinch while pilfering their wallet over the sound of their snoring. Two hundred bucks, or two thousand, she didn't care. It was all tax free.

Again, we stayed too long. I was anxious to depart, but Joy would have none of it. She was ringing the cash register every night and playing like a rock star every day. I was nothing but a body guard, tagging along in case some seventy year old got too frisky. We'd dropped the charter fishing scam a few towns back. This part of Florida was less fishing and more retirees. I urged Joy to quit, leave this place and run for home. We argued about it again, finally settling on one more score before ending it. I wish I'd have fought harder. The decision to stay one more day was the biggest mistake either of us would ever make.

Disaster

It was a typical, sunny, south Florida day. We were walking arm in arm on a busy sidewalk in South Miami. The people-watching was excellent. We were visiting bars and planning our angle of attack for the coming evening. There was one last victim to be fleeced. We planned to leave for Cayo Costa in the morning. We were in our own little world amongst the thousands of other pedestrians. My guard was down. I didn't see him.

Suddenly, Joy stopped in her tracks. She hid behind me.
"What is it?" I asked.
"It's him," she answered.
"Who?" I said.

"Joe, it's Jerk-Off Joe," she replied. "God, Breeze, he's got a gun."

I found him. He was barely thirty feet away, standing in the middle of the sidewalk. His right arm hung by his side. There was a pistol in his hand, pointed at the ground. My hesitation ended when his arm started to rise. I broke free of Joy's grasp and ran right at him. I didn't think. I didn't have time to figure out the best course of action. I just reacted.

As I sprinted towards him, I saw the gun come up. He was stoic and steady. He leveled and aimed. I pushed my boat bum legs like a football linebacker, churning hard. I was ten yards away when I heard the first shot. I didn't feel a thing. Just before I reached him he fired again. Still, I felt nothing. I lowered my shoulder and plowed into his mid-section with all the strength I could muster.

I felt the air leave him. I heard the gun clatter across the concrete. I was on top of him and he was winded. I started pounding his face with both fists. My right held up fine, but I felt something crack in my left fist. I abandoned the punches and started slamming his head on the curb, with my good hand. His face was mush. The back of his head had a good-sized gash and blood poured out of it. Onlookers pulled me off. One of them had the pistol. If they spoke I didn't hear them. Gunshots rang in my ears, and my own blood was pulsing in my head.

I turned to find Joy. She was down on the ground. Her chest was bright red. Her skin was unnaturally pale. Joe hadn't aimed at me. He had come for Joy and fired at her in spite of my charge. His bullets, one of them at least, had found their target. I ran to her and cradled her in my lap. Tears soaked her face. Her hands were on her wound and covered in blood.

Fresh blood has a metallic smell. It's coppery and pungent. When that blood is flowing from someone you care about, the odor sticks with you for a long time. It was all so unreal, as if I was floating above, watching myself hold a dying woman in my arms. She wouldn't, or couldn't, look directly at me. She was staring straight ahead, trembling.

"Please not yet," she whispered. "I can't die yet."

"Hang in there," I said. "Help is on the way."

I heard the sirens approaching. I was vaguely aware of all the people standing around us, watching. This was a common occurrence in Miami. These people were hardened to watching their fellow humans die in the street. An older woman handed me her scarf, which I pressed into the wound. It was saturated in seconds.

"I never told you that I love you," she said.

"It's okay, Joy. We'll have plenty of time for that later."

We did not have time. She coughed up blood and tightened her body. When the spasm relaxed, she was gone. I felt the life drain out of her. I hugged her and held her close to me. I closed my eyes tightly to hold back the tears. *Lord, please forgive her. Take her home to a better place. She didn't deserve this.*

I laid her down with the scarf under her head. I stood and looked around. Police officers were taking eyewitness accounts. Paramedics were loading Joe onto a gurney. I could hear more sirens approaching. A familiar instinct kicked in. I ran. I was covered in Joy's blood. My hands were battered and bleeding. I had tears running down my cheeks. I must have been one hell of a sight, but no one tried to stop me. I heard a cop yell for me, but I ignored him. I did what I had always done, run from trouble. There was a big old basket of trouble back there. *Run, Breeze, Run.*

The boat was anchored north of the Venetian Causeway Bridge, near the Harbor Yacht Club. The dinghy was tied up at a dock outside a launch ramp. The ramp was part of a park. The park also housed the Miami Beach Marine Patrol. I couldn't make a bloody, mad dash past the cop shop to get to my dinghy. Instead, I cut across the beach. I kicked off my flip flops and ripped off the bloody shirt. I ran down to the shoreline and out into the water. I dove and swam underwater as far as I could. I came up gasping, and starting stroking for deeper water. I swam parallel to shore until the dock and launch ramp came into view. I wasn't a great swimmer. My lungs couldn't get enough air and my arms were burning.

Finally, I reached water shallow enough to stand. I made my way to the dinghy, but was too tired to climb aboard. I untied it from the dock, and dragged it into shallower water. Once aboard, I fired up the old Mercury outboard. I looked back for any pursuers, but saw none. I hit the throttle and sped off towards *Leap of Faith*. Once again, she was all I had left.

On deck, I stripped out of my shorts and boxers. Most of the blood had washed off my skin while I swam. I scrubbed hard anyway. I put the bloody clothes in a bag, added some lead sinkers, and dropped it overboard. Once I was cleaned up, I grabbed a beer and sat down. The adrenaline that had been driving me subsided. I felt like those clothes, sinking down into the depths. Joy was gone. She had said, "Please, not yet." Please not yet... but death took her and she was gone.

As I was prone to do, I decided to blame myself. I should have known better. Hell, I DID know better, but went along with her anyway. Back when she had made herself vulnerable to me, after her husband had beaten her up, I promised to keep her safe. Jerk-Off Joe had drifted far from our minds. We weren't prepared. We hadn't been alert. We had taken our freedom for granted. It had gotten one of us killed.

I was still alive. I had survived yet again. I had to figure out what to do next. Joy wasn't coming with me. She would never see Pelican Bay again. I hoped that there was a bar in heaven, where she could flirt with angels for free drinks.

Person of Interest

I was driving myself crazy, alone on the boat. I paced back and forth, making myself miserable. I was always good at feeling guilty. I needed to get drunk, but there was only a few beers left aboard. I decided to go to a bar.

I walked a few side streets until I found what I was looking for. I entered a quiet place designed for hardcore drinkers. There was no music. A single television hung above the center of the bar. The news was on. There I was, covered in blood, leaving Joy's body lying there on the sidewalk. There was Joe, lying on a gurney, being wheeled to a waiting ambulance. A bobble-headed blond stood next to the blood stain and described the man in the video as a "person of interest".

The shooter was in stable condition. An eyewitness described his actions as cold-blooded murder. Another described the dude who beat up the shooter as almost a hero.
"He was fearless, man," he said. "He ran right into the fire, but he was too late to save the lady. Don't know why he ran away."
Almost a hero. Ran away. Fearless. Ran away. I couldn't make sense of it myself. I ordered a glass of rum. The bartender gave me a quizzical look.

"You heard me, barkeep," I said. "A glass of rum, neat."

I drank the rum and a few more beers. It numbed me. The pain turned to anger. I felt it best to leave the bar before I did something stupid. I made it back to the boat and flopped down on the bed. I drifted off to sleep with a montage of women in my head. Laura, Andi, Yolanda, and Joy haunted me in my sleep. They weren't all dead, but they were all gone. I'd driven them off, or they had died. Whatever it was about women, I was doing it wrong.

When I sobered up, I began to regret my decision to run. Not because I wanted to deal with a bunch of cops and reporters, but because I had abandoned Joy's body. I wondered what would happen to her. I decided to find out. I called the coroner's office.

"Are you a member of the immediate family, sir?" the lady asked.

"No, just a friend," I answered.

"I can't release detailed information to anyone but family and law enforcement," she proclaimed.

"I'd like to make arrangements for her," I replied.

"Her in-laws have already called," she stated. "She's being shipped to Houston tomorrow."

"Thank you," I said, as I hung up.

As I understood it, Joe's parents were wealthy. It would be no big deal for them to do right by their daughter in-law. I doubted Joy would approve of being buried in the family plot, but it was out of my hands now. At least I wouldn't be carrying her ashes around, along with Laura's.

I really didn't know what to do next. I'd lost all ambition. I was rudderless. I went to the bar every night and drank too much. I watched the news for any new information on Jerk-Off Joe and myself. Joe had been transferred from the hospital, to a mental health facility. His family had hired a whole team of high-profile lawyers. Based on their interviews with the press, an insanity plea was being cultivated. Joy had left him. She had emptied his bank account and ran away. He couldn't deal with it. He snapped. His grief was too great. Two old drunks at the bar vehemently disagreed with the manicured attorney. I kept my mouth shut. The videos were of poor quality, taken from surveillance cameras. So far, no one had recognized me.

It dawned on me that Joy's boat was still anchored in Fort Myers Beach. I'd have to do something about that. I finally had a reason to pull up and leave this wretched city. Adios, Miami, and good riddance. This city was American culture on steroids, with a Cuban flair. I hated it. The noise was continual and oppressive. The traffic never stopped. Loud motorcycles competed with diesel trucks on the decibel meter. The eateries were all cling and clang, like never-ending cocktail parties. The music was fluff that clogged the ears further. Radios, TV, people everywhere, horns honking, jets overhead - it was enough to drive me bonkers.

It brought to mind a passage written by John D. MacDonald in *A Deadly Shade of Gold*.

"There is a spurious vitality about all this noise. But under it, you can sense another more significant vitality. It has been somewhat beaten down of late. The bell ringers and flag fondlers have been busy peddling their notion that to make America strong, we must march in close and obedient ranks, to the sound of their tin whistle. The life-adjustment educators, in strange alliance with the hucksters of consumer goods, have been doing their damnest to make us all think alike, look alike, smell alike, and die alike, amidst all the pocket-queek of unserviceable home appliances, our armpits astringent, nasal passages clear, insurance programs adequate, sex life satisfying, retirement assured, medical plan comprehensive, hair free of dandruff, time payments manageable, waistline firm, bowels open.

But the other vitality is still there, that rancorous sardonic, wonderful insistence on the right to dissent, to question, to object, to raise holy hell and, in the direst extremity, to laugh the self-appointed squad leaders off the face of the earth with great whoops of dirty disdainful glee. Suppress friction and a machine runs fine. Suppress friction, and a society runs down.

I wanted to object. All those fakers scurrying around Miami had it all wrong. What was important to them meant nothing at all to me. Their idea of counter-culture was tattoos and piercings. My life was authentically counter to modern culture. I wasn't real happy at that moment, but I was my own man. I had not conformed. Losing everything that was important to me would not make me join the teeming masses of braying sheep.

My status as a person of interest had not caused anyone to recognize me. I figured that I'd be even safer on the other side of the state. Joy and I had saved up a good chunk of money, enough to last me a long time if I was careful with it. It was time to move. I carefully considered what route to take back to the west coast of Florida. Going back up to Stuart and crossing the waterway there was the safest bet. I dreaded those locks, and it was a lot longer route than skirting the keys and crossing Florida Bay. The southern crossing would put me in close proximity to Bald Mark's turf. The northern choice was clearly the right choice, regardless of the inconvenience.

I chose the southern route. I wanted to get home and I wanted to do it quickly. Flirting with danger might sharpen me up. I'd lost a bit of my situational awareness lately. I could make it from Key Largo to the Everglades in one long day. I'd only be vulnerable for a few hours as I passed Tavernier. Only an incredible coincidence would cause me to run into Bald Mark, or horrible luck.

I staged at No Name Key for the night. It was a lousy anchorage. I didn't sleep well for fear of the anchor dragging. I was tense and unsettled. I thought about Joy. Her absence was palpable. I tried to harden myself to the loss. I gave up trying to sleep well before dawn.

I took a small chance by pulling up anchor before sunrise. The problem with running the next stretch of the ICW was the presence of lobster pots. I knew that I could cut through Tarpon Basin, off Key Largo, and make it most of the way to Islamorada, before they got too thick. By then the sun would be up and I could spot them. This put me beyond Tavernier in the early morning. Fishermen would be the only boats I'd encounter.

Everything went as planned. I used the old yacht channel to cross Florida Bay. Flamingo was barely visible to my starboard, as I neared Cape Sable. I knew these waters. I easily skirted the shoals and ran north along the Everglades National Park. I dropped anchor just inside the mouth of Little Shark River, without another boat in sight. I slept well, and remembered no dreams. I woke refreshed. I left at first light, taking my coffee up on the bridge. I ran *Leap of Faith* hard all day, to reach Goodland by dark. I entered the Ten Thousand Islands at Coon Key. I veered off the main channel just west of Goodland's harbor and approached Sugar Bay. Slowing to a crawl, I eased over a shallow bar at the entrance. I found good water beyond the bar. No one would ever see me here. I could relax. Tomorrow I'd be in Fort Myers Beach.

All alone in a hidden cove surrounded by mangroves, I took stock of my life. I'd bounced back and forth between poverty and riches. I'd shared wonderful relationships and I'd been alone. I'd had some good fortune, and some really bad luck. I'd made a few good decisions, but they seemed to be outnumbered by the bad choices that I'd made. What was I supposed to do now? I had money to live, but I didn't have a life. All purpose and ambition had been sucked out of me. I was a lost soul, wandering about in a sea of despair.

A buzzing hoard of mosquitoes snapped me out of my trance. I retreated indoors and closed up for the night. *Go to bed, Breeze. You can feel sorry for yourself tomorrow.*

I dreamt that I was a white knight. My steed was *Leap of Faith*. I traveled the Seven Seas, saving the world from evil.

Another Adventure

I found Joy's vessel where we had left it. I anchored nearby. When I boarded *Another Adventure,* Joy's death came rushing back at me. Clothes were tossed about randomly. Books were stacked at the nav station in a haphazard manner. Ball caps and bikini tops hung randomly from assorted hooks. Her personality was evident in the stuff scattered about the salon. I hadn't really spent a lot of time on her boat. Mostly, when we were together, it was aboard my vessel. I felt like an intruder. What to do with her stuff?

One-legged Beth yelled from outside.
"Ahoy, Breeze. You in there?"
"Permission to board, Beth," I answered.

She filled me in on what she knew. She and the guys knew that I was the infamous person of interest. They saw the news about Joy's death on TV. Some of the boaters that hung out at the Upper Deck figured it was me as well. Everyone had been greatly saddened by the news, but the story faded quickly from the headlines here.

"What are we going to do with her boat?" Beth asked.

"You are going to sell it," I answered.

"Me?"

"Yes, you," I said. "You will be Joy, for the purposes of showing and selling it."

"You know, Breeze," she started. "My boat ain't much. It don't even run or have sails."

"You, Diver Dan, and Robin will split the money three ways," I said. "Get Dan to go over the engine. Have Robin air out the sails. You clean up in here. Everybody gets paid."

We shook hands on the deal and went our separate ways. Beth headed over towards Dan's boat. I went to the library to use a computer. I listed *Another Adventure* for sale on Craigslist and Boat Trader. I asked for seventy grand. We'd take sixty. That would mean twenty grand each to my backwater friends. They'd been Joy's friends too. The money would make a big difference in their lives.

When I walked into the bar that night, everyone looked as if they'd seen a ghost. I stopped, put my arms up and addressed all of them.

"What?" I asked. "No welcome back Breeze?"

The barmaid, Jennifer, was the first to speak.

"We're all real sorry about Joy," she said. "We've been worried about you too. Not every day we see one of our own on the news."

"I'd like to stay out of the news from now on," I said. "I'd appreciate if all of you would stay quiet as to my whereabouts."

She addressed everyone at the bar.

"Is Breeze safe up here with us?" she asked them. "Are we all family here? Or is one of you going to rat him out? Anyone who squeals won't be welcome here. Understood?"

Everyone muttered and nodded agreement. Jennifer and I hadn't really been close. I had kept a pretty low profile. It was nice of her to step up on my behalf. I suddenly noticed that underneath the sweat and beer stains, she was pretty cute. Joy's presence had blinded me when I was in here before.

Over the next several days, the gang cleaned up Joy's boat and made it ready to show prospective buyers. Beth handled some calls, half of which were from brokers wanting to list the boat. There was a slip available at the Matanzas Inn Marina, so I made arrangements to move *Another Adventure* to the docks there. We hung a For Sale sign on her, and Beth moved aboard to look after things.

There wasn't much for me to do. I spent my afternoons lounging around the pool at the Lighthouse Resort. I spent happy hour with my new friends at the Upper Deck. I tipped Jennifer heavily and tried to engage her in conversation when she wasn't too busy. I still hadn't figured out what to do with my life. I was getting restless. I knew from experience, that when I got restless, I tended to make my worst decisions. I'd have to be on the lookout for whatever temptation was about to present itself. That didn't necessarily mean I'd do the right thing. It would just be nice to know what I was getting myself into next.

My answer showed up a few days later. It came via water taxi.

On board was the last person I thought I'd ever see, or wanted to see. Bald Mark stood on deck with his arms crossed. His smooth skull was glistening with sweat. His biceps were as big as ever. He was smiling. I grabbed my shotgun and racked the slide in full view of the driver and his passenger. Bald Mark raised his hands in the air.

"Truce," he said. "I come in peace."

"Why do I find that hard to believe?" I said.

"We had a little misunderstanding," he said. "I think we should clear that up. I've gained some new knowledge of the circumstances. Maybe I was wrong about you. This is your chance to tell your side of the story."

I considered his offer and tried to gauge his intentions. He put his arms down and opened his palms towards me.

"You have my word," he said. "No violence. I'm just here to talk."

"Okay, come aboard," I said. "We'll talk."

I didn't like being in such close proximity to this man, but my curiosity got the better of me. He told me the story Enrique had given him about our encounter. It was embellished. Enrique had tried to rape my pretty Cuban passenger and I bashed his head in with a hammer. He had told us that Mark would rape her too, and that she would be dumped in Little Havana when the whole gang was finished with her. I'd crossed Bald Mark by disabling his man, and running off with the girl. He wanted me dead. Enrique had told a different story.

Slowly, small details started to circulate. Enrique's story became suspicious. Then Enrique was arrested, for trying to kill me. He quickly turned on Bald Mark to try to save his ass. Bald Mark eventually figured out that he had been lied to.

"Why would you think I'd sanction rape of the general's daughter?" he asked. "I'd be stupid to piss off my Cuban gift horse."

"I guess you had to be there," I said. "He convinced Yolanda. The rape was real enough. I did what I had to do, at the time."

"You could have come to me right then," he said. "I'd have handled him."

"Your other men were still out there in the fast boats," I said. "I believed you would kill me. All I wanted to do was keep the girl safe."

"What did you do with her?" he asked.

"She's safe," I said. "You won't find her. She's got a chance for a decent life."

"You took out a bigger and meaner man. You managed to elude me and my men. You took her someplace safe without anyone knowing. You end up in Miami with a dead blonde in your arms. The cops never make you. I obviously underestimated your abilities."

"So what do we do now?" I asked.

He asked for a beer and we went inside to sit down. He seemed thoughtful, considering what he would say next. We were both silent for a minute.

"I want you to work for me," he said.

"You have got to be joking," I said.

"No joke. I'm going to go on a little taxpayer paid vacation at a minimum security country club soon," he said. "My crew is in jail. The DEA has taken my boats. I want you to bring in the product while I'm gone."

"Even if I wanted to, I don't know anything about running your business," I said. "I just know boats."

"I've enlisted Tiki Terry to handle the books and distribution," he said. "All you gotta do is bring in the goods. You'll be working with a friend."

"Compensation?" I asked.

"Fifty grand per haul," he answered. "I should be out in less than a year. After that, if you want to stay you can. If you want to leave, no hard feelings."

"How much time do I have to decide?" I asked.

"A month probably," he answered. "My lawyer will let me know when I report."

"I tell you what," I started. "I'm going to seriously consider this, but I need some time."

"Here's my new number," he said, handing me a card. "The feds are listening to the old one."

He called for the water taxi and we shook hands. The look he gave me seemed to convey sincerity. It was a good trick for someone with black eyes.

Escape

After Bald Mark left, I headed straight for the bar. It wasn't happy hour yet, but I needed more beer. Jennifer was behind the bar. Only two other customers sat there, watching the early news. That's when I saw him.

The story was about the recent escape of a patient from a mental hospital near Houston, Texas. It was Jerk-Off Joe. The newsman recapped the story of Joy's death in Miami. I had tried hard to forget that day. Now it all came back to me, and Joe was on the loose. This could not stand.

"Holy shit, Breeze," said Jennifer. "You watching this?"

"I see it," I answered. "It's a hell of a thing."

"Are you okay?" she asked. "What's going through your mind?"

"I'm thinking about finding him, and killing him," I said.

"Be serious, Breeze," she said. "The cops don't know where he went. No leads."

I thought I knew where he would go. I remembered his boat. No one knew he owned it, not even his parents. It was fully stocked for a doomsday scenario. He would go to his boat. I was going to Texas. I'd done nothing to make amends for Joy. I was floundering with no purpose. Now I had one. I'd hunt that fucker down. I threw a twenty on the bar and say goodbye to Jennifer. Flirting with her would have to wait for another time. I had plans to make.

Things had changed dramatically in the past twenty four hours. Not one, but two spectacular revelations had presented themselves. I wasn't being hunted by Bald Mark. I could choose to partner with him if I wished. Joy's killer was free, at least temporarily. His escape had become my escape. Yesterday, I was in a funk. Today, I was energized. I might be the only person alive who knew where he might hide. I could call the police, but that's not how I operated.

Back on board I hauled out my guide books and charts. I had a four year old copy of Dozier's Southern Waterway Guide, but no charts outside of Florida. I'd never been north of Tampa Bay. A few quick calculations revealed that an open Gulf Crossing to Galveston was roughly seven hundred miles. I was not prepared for such a journey. Neither was *Miss Leap*. I'd have to go up the ICW as far as Anclote Key. I could jump off from there to Carrabelle.

I had a lot to do to get ready, and I was anxious to start. I took on fuel and water at Moss Marine on the way out. I could have gone much further, but I stopped in Pelican Bay. I didn't know how this adventure was going to turn out. I wanted to spend a few hours in the only place on Earth I considered home. I could sit down with the guidebook and map out the rest of my route to Galveston.

Securely at anchor, I fished out what was left of Laura's ashes and sat down to think. When she was alive, I could always count on her to provide sensible input. I stared at the battered little canister waiting for inspiration. None came. I was truly on my own. In my mind, I worked through possible scenarios for my eventual meeting with Joy's killer. What I really wanted to do was put a bullet in his head. Could I?

I couldn't concentrate on the charts. I knew the next portion of the trip pretty well, so I gave up my study. I'd figure it out along the way. I popped open a beer and carried Laura out on the back deck, like I'd done so many times. I sat in silence and waited for sunset. I tried to feel her presence, but it just wouldn't come. I supposed my unresolved grief for Joy was interfering. I knew what the resolution was. I'd find Joe and bring him to justice, one way or another.

I pulled out of Pelican Bay, crossed the Boca Grande Pass, and motored north on the inside of Gasparilla Island. I had to wait a few minutes for the swing bridge, which wasn't unusual. The next few bridges had high enough clearance for me to go under without opening them. The Blackburn Point swing bridge opened on demand. From there it was an easy shot to Anna Maria Island. I pulled into the field of derelict boats at Bradenton Beach late in the afternoon. Deciding to have a few drinks in town, I took the dinghy in to shore. I found a bum sleeping on a bench near the trash cans. I stood on the corner and looked down the block, trying to decide on a bar. From across the street, a guy came out of the trailer park bar with a case of beer. He asked if I wanted it. The delivery guy ruled it out of date and said he couldn't sell it. It was mine if I wanted it. It was still cold. I took the case of beer and returned to the bench with the sleeping bum. I nudged him awake. He sat up and gave me a strange look, like I'd disturbed his beauty sleep.

"Hey buddy," I said. "You want some beer? It's still cold."

I got another weird look. I couldn't tell if the old guy was all there or not. I took a beer out of the box, opened it, and handed it to him. He drank from the bottle and spoke.

"Thanks," he said. "I could really use a cold beer."

Instead of going to a bar, I sat there on that bench and drank free beer with a vagrant. He didn't talk much, which was fine by me. Eventually, I got up to go.

"You ever get some rum you come back and see me," he said. "I'm here most days. I could use a glass of rum too."

"I'll do that," I promised.

I went back to *Leap of Faith* to look over charts once again. I had another day's run to get up near Anclote Key. I decided I'd anchor off Three Rooker Bar the next day. I steered clear of the huge tankers transiting Tampa Bay and continued north. I passed St. Petersburg, Clearwater, and Dunedin. I got the anchor down that afternoon just before a thunderstorm hit. I used the last of the daylight to plot a course across the open Gulf to Carrabelle, on the western edge of Florida's Big Bend. It would take me about twenty hours. I decided to leave at noon the next day, hoping to make landfall at first light.

I checked the weather report. It wasn't perfect, but I was okay with it. I couldn't help but think that traveling was so much less hassle without a woman on board. I could deal with four to six foot seas no problem. I didn't mind bashing and slamming a little. The boat could handle even more. She wasn't really in trouble unless the seas exceeded ten feet. I hoped not to see any waves that big.

We nosed out into the Gulf and I said a silent prayer to the Gods of the sea for a safe crossing. All the gauges were within normal operating range. The engine purred. *Let's do this Miss Leap.* It got a little bumpy, but I actually enjoyed it. I always felt inspired out on the open water. It was my boat and I against the elements. She'd never let me down.

It was barely dawn when I approached the mouth of the St. Marks River. I had full daylight by the time I neared Carrabelle. I found a place to anchor just inside the hook of the west end of Dog Island. The worst part of this journey was done. I could hop in and out along the Gulf Coast the rest of the way, with plenty of rivers and bays to seek shelter in, if necessary. I'd blazed a new trail, crossing water I'd never seen. It felt good. I spent some time checking on the boats systems. Each check or maintenance item was goodwill in the bank in my mind.

Once I finished my chores, I realized how tired I was. It had been a long ride. I didn't even crack the rum bottle. I just laid down my head and drifted off into a deep sleep. I had the strangest dream. It was like seeing a slide show. There was nothing but still shots, a few seconds each. I saw Laura. I saw Andi, Yolanda, and Joy. All four women were in an endless loop of photographs. It lacked any emotion or feeling. It had a forensic feel to it. Not quite mug shots, but not glamour shots either. I had no clue what it might mean.

I woke late, but not too late to make the next run in daylight hours. I felt refreshed and ready to face what may come. I retraced my course down the river, into St. George Sound. I took the inside route through Apalachicola Bay and made it to the Apalachicola Municipal Marina to get fuel before they closed. I didn't see a good place to anchor, so I continued on until I reached the split of Jackson River and Saul Creek. The water was very deep, almost thirty feet, but the place was very well protected. I set the anchor and settled in for the night.

Over the next two days, I made brief stopovers in Destin and Gulf Shores, Alabama. Everything was going fine. The boat was fine. I was fine. It was almost too easy. This was nothing like island hopping in the Caribbean, where each trip was potentially dangerous, even life-threatening. Near Gulf Shores, I anchored in Roberts Bayou, which some folks called "Pirates Cove". The entrance was very narrow, but I slid in with no difficulties. I had yet to go to shore since leaving Bradenton Beach. I decided to put the dinghy in and went to get some dinner at Pirates Cove Marina Restaurant.

Next I crossed Mobile Bay to Dauphin Island. After that I was in Mississippi. I wanted to bypass New Orleans for a fast run to the west. I went out around the Chandeleur Islands in shallow water and found a mine field of oil platforms and wrecks. The channel was well marked, but it ended up being a very long run to Venice. At that point, I had a decision to make. I was itching to have my showdown. I wanted to be in Texas as fast as possible. I sat down with the charts again and laid a course across the near-shore Gulf for Galveston. It was long, but doable. All I needed was good weather. I didn't get it.

I made it as far as Port Arthur when a tropical depression formed in the Gulf. It was forecasted to become Tropical Storm Bill within twenty four hours. It looked to make landfall well to the west of Galveston, but it would stir up the offshore waters for days. I had no choice but to seek shelter and lay low for a few days. I found a place called Stingaree Marina and pulled up to the fuel dock. I got the diesel and water tanks topped off, and took a slip for two days. They had a restaurant upstairs serving seafood. As I ate, I tried to visualize how it would go down if and when I found my target.

I had beaten the crap out of him once, but I suspected it would be different this time. He'd be on alert for pending trouble. He'd be solely focused on his survival. Back in Miami, he'd been solely focused on killing Joy. He sacrificed self-defense in order to get his shots off. I wouldn't have such an advantage this time. The only plan I could come up with, was to find him, stake him out, and see what opportunity presented itself. I'd improvise. I'd think of something when the time came. Winging it, was my specialty.

The storm made landfall that night near Matagorda. I decided to give it another day to settle down. I had dinner at Little Chihuahuas. They served me a heaping helping of honey shrimp enchiladas which I chased down with a few cold Dos Equis beers. I was only a day away from my destination. I could feel my adrenaline levels tick up a notch. I had my mission. I was very close to carrying it out.

It was about a fifty mile run from Sabine Pass to Galveston. I ran out from the jetties for a mile, then I turned to two hundred, forty-two degrees magnetic. That heading kept me out of the shipping fairways and in thirty foot of water. There was very little wind, but the storm left me with some soft swells of about four feet. The last leg of my trip was almost pleasant. A bit of nervousness put an edge on my mood, and prevented me from completely enjoying a nice day at sea.

The entrance to Galveston Bay seemed straightforward. The long jetties were almost a mile apart. As I turned into the channel, a strong ebb tide slowed me down. A following sea was creating serious rollers and cresting seas running in from the deeper Gulf. There was commercial traffic everywhere. *Leap of Faith* beat and slashed her way towards Galveston Bay. It was uncomfortable until we finally cleared the Coast Guard station just inside the bay's entrance. We passed the ferry docks and aimed for Galveston Channel. Passing Seawolf Park, I saw a large WWII-era submarine tied to the docks.

Jerk-Off Joe kept his boat at the Galveston Yacht Club, according to Joy. I passed it by, and continued up the channel until I found an anchorage. The current was severely swift, so I deployed two anchors in the Bahamian style. Traffic was heavy, but I was well off the wide channel and riding on the anchor wasn't uncomfortable. I stayed with the boat for another hour to be sure the anchors were well set. Once I was satisfied, I took the dinghy to explore.

I'm coming for you, Joe. You will pay for what you did to Joy.

Galveston

Pelican Island blocked the winds off Galveston Bay, so I had a smooth dinghy ride to shore. I couldn't simply drive into Joe's marina. I made some simple assumptions about how he would stay hidden. He would most likely have drawn curtains or blackened windows to block the view of passersby. I also had to assume he'd have a way to look out, without being detected. He knew what I looked like.

I found a dock a few blocks away and walked down the street to the yacht club entrance. There was a restaurant with an upstairs terrace overlooking the marina. It would become my new hangout. I got a beer from the bar and walked over to the railing. I had a nice vantage point to inspect the boats in their slips. I saw several big Carvers, but I couldn't read the names from up there. I needed to walk the docks. How could I do it without Joe spotting me?

I took a table that still gave me a partial view of the yacht basin. I ate slowly, and kept looking around, observing. Fishermen were returning to the ramp next door. I noticed a few of the guides wearing those cloth things that covered their ears, nose and face. It was to prevent skin cancer. Many of the guides in Florida dressed the same way. They wore long-sleeved shirts, lightweight long pants, and face coverings.

The next day I walked the strip until I found what I was looking for. I needed an upscale pro shop that sold the type of clothing I had seen the night before at the ramp. I purchased everything I needed. My new duds would conceal my identity as I searched for Joe's boat. I went back to my boat to change. This time I took the dinghy right up to the dock at the boat ramp. I asked how the fishing was. I shot the shit with an old guy at the fuel dock whose skin was the consistency of dried leather. I told him I was looking to buy a yacht, and that I was partial to big Carvers. He pointed out a few in the marina, but said he didn't think they were for sale. He didn't mind if I took a look.

I found it at the far end of the marina. *Fifty Shades* hadn't been washed or waxed in a while. It had a small aft cockpit with a sliding entrance door to the interior. The side windows were tinted dark black. The slider had vertical blinds blocking my view of the inside. Joe could easily peek out through them, though. I continued down the dock and pretended to check out a few more boats. Finally, I'd seen enough. I left the marina and waiting for nightfall.

I went back upstairs to the bar after dark. I knew which boat to watch now. I sat there until closing. Nothing happened. No lights or sign of movement were evident. If he was on that boat, he was doing a good job of hiding his presence. I came back and renewed my vigil the next night, and the night after that. I didn't see a thing. On the fourth night, something may have happened. I thought I saw a concentrated beam of light inside Joe's boat. It could have been a flashlight, but I couldn't be positive. It was on and off in a flash. Was it a reflection from somewhere else? Was it evidence that he was onboard? I just couldn't be certain.

On the fifth night I saw something else. The vertical blinds moved. I was positive. There was no wake in the marina at the time. There was nothing to disturb the blinds. It wasn't much, but they definitely moved, ever so slightly. Jerk-Off Joe was sneaking a peak outside. I'd been right. I knew he'd run to his boat to hide. I had him now. I just needed a plan to draw him out. I went back to my boat to think it over. I had a good lay of the land. I knew where he was. He didn't know I was there.

Before falling asleep, I began to have second thoughts. Should I call the police? Should I bash my way in, with gun blazing? Could I sabotage his vessel, in order to draw him out? Dozens of possibilities ran through my mind, but I couldn't settle on a course of action. I was too close to quit now, though. I decided to sleep on it. I tipped the rum bottle a few times to help me doze off.

I walked the historic downtown strand the next day, considering my options. I strolled through the historic district past the Victorian buildings, museums and cafes. I ate lunch at Fisherman's Wharf on Pier 21. I went down to the Texas Seaport Museum, and took a tour of the tall ship Elissa. Before turning back, I checked out the aquarium and tropical rain forest at Moody Gardens. On the way back, I saw a pizza delivery guy ring a doorbell on Harborside Drive. It gave me an idea.

After dark, I ordered a pizza. I had it delivered to the front gate of the yacht club. I offered the delivery guy twenty bucks for his Domino's hat. He accepted. Down at the marina docks, I told the guard I had a delivery for slip D-24. I said the guy was handicapped, and couldn't come to the gate. He let me through. I walked like I was in a hurry until I reached Joe's boat. I hopped right aboard like I belonged there and yelled out.

"Domino's Pizza," I said. "You ordered a large pepperoni?"

He fell for it just enough. He cracked open the sliding door to tell me I had the wrong boat. Before he could speak the words, I had one hand and one foot inside the crack. I shoved the door open with a violent thrust. With my other hand I shoved the pizza box into his face. I could feel the power of my anger surge within me. I had caught him off-guard. He didn't expect a violent attack from a dumb pizza delivery guy who couldn't find the right boat. I had gone through this in my mind a dozen times. Each time I overpowered him right at the door. The element of surprise gave me the advantage. I'd smash him to bits and it would all be over.

That's not how it worked out.

Just inside the slider, two steps led down to the salon floor. We both fell inward and my advantage was lost. As I fell I saw that he was holding a gun. I chopped at his wrist on my way down and the gun went flying. We wrestled in warm pizza. He managed to come out on top and started flailing away with his fists. I blocked most of his blows, but a few got through. He was much stronger than I anticipated. I felt honest fear at that moment in time. This had all gone terribly wrong. I saw him glance towards the gun. I had to do something quick, but I couldn't get off a good punch, without letting my guard down.

He connected a solid blow to my temple that caused my ears to ring. I saw a flash of light behind my eyes. That's when he made his move for the gun. I recovered in time to trip him with my foot. He went down a few feet short of the pistol. I was on top of him in an instant. He tried to rise, but I rammed his forehead into a corner table. It slowed him enough for me to reach the gun first. He grabbed me from behind. Out of instinct, I swung the weapon at his head. I scored a direct hit between his eyes. He went down. I kicked him hard between the legs, but he barely flinched. He was out cold.

I stood over him with the gun in my right hand. Tomato sauce mixed with blood, dripped down my arm. I looked at the weapon. Finding the safety, I clicked it off. I knelt down behind him and put the barrel against the back of his head. I hesitated. My hand was trembling. The longer I held my stance, the more I shook. I imagined my little devil telling me to blow his brains out. *Do it, Breeze. Waste the fucker.*

I couldn't do it. I didn't have what it took to deliberately take a man's life. He deserved to die, but it wouldn't be at my hand. Still, I had won. I had tracked him down, and defeated him. I put the safety back on and looked around the cabin. I found some pieces of rope hanging on a peg. I used them to tie up my victim. I made it as uncomfortable as I could. I tied his hands behind his back. I roped his feet together. I tied his feet to his hands. I tightened up the whole mess as much as I could. He moaned softly. When he came to he wouldn't be able to move at all. Satisfied with my efforts, I left him to fill a bucket with water.

I returned and poured it over his head. I wanted him awake. After he finished coughing and sputtering, I turned his face to me.

"My name is Breeze, asshole," I said. "I beat you in Miami, and I beat you here on your own boat. I just want you to know who the man is, in this relationship. You took Joy's life, and now I'm taking yours."

He begged for his life. He cried real tears. It was pathetic. When he started to blame it all on Joy, I'd heard enough. I put him back to sleep with the butt of his own gun.

I put the gun on the galley counter and used his sink to clean myself up. I had a nasty cut over my left eye, and more than a few bumps on my head. The Breeze that looked back at me in the mirror had a wild look in his eyes. He looked crazy. I tried to calm myself. Adrenaline was a strange thing. When it leaves your body, there is a hangover left behind. All the strength ran out of me. I needed to get off that damned boat. I had to call the police. Joe was stirring in the salon. It was time to go.

I closed the slider behind me and stepped onto the dock. I saw no one else moving about. I gathered myself together and started walking back towards the gate. I nodded to the guard and headed for the parking lot. As I approached a hedgerow that surrounded the property, a man stepped out of the bushes with his gun drawn. He held up a badge. He told me to put my hands up.

"Detective Pace," he said. "And you are?"

"The name's Breeze," I told him.

"Full name, wise guy," he demanded.

"Meade Edwin Breeze," I said. "Florida boat bum."

"I've been watching that boat for three weeks," he said. "I haven't seen a thing, until tonight. You want to tell me what just went down?"

"I was on my way to call it in," I said. "Why didn't you just raid the boat?"

"No warrant," he said. "I found the paper trail, but the judge didn't buy it. I take it you're not the pizza delivery guy."

"I was the angel of vengeance twenty minutes ago," I said. "I'm kind of sapped now though. Mind if I sit down?"

"How'd you know about the boat?" he asked.

"I had some inside information from a certain deceased woman," I replied.

"You were the guy with her in Miami," he said. "The press will eat this up."

He led me to his car and locked me inside. I watched as he returned to the marina. Within minutes I could hear the sirens. I looked on as two uniformed cops led Joe up the ramp in handcuffs. News vans arrived. Crews set up cameras and reporters talked into microphones. I wanted to lie down and go to sleep. When detective Pace returned, he said I'd have to make a statement downtown. At the station, it didn't take long for someone to figure out that I was on probation in Florida. I spent the night in the Galveston City Jail.

Someone brought me coffee in the morning. I was told that the lawn and parking lot were full of media people wanting to ask me some questions. I made calls to Taylor, and Miranda. They advised me to talk to the press, in order to gain sympathy for violating my probation. I was a hero, they told me. I didn't feel much like a hero. My head hurt and I had zero energy. Detective Pace showed up and told me I was free to go.

I was mobbed as soon as I left the building. The local reporters were in my face. Good Morning America wanted to fly me to New York. Fox News wanted an exclusive. There was a cab waiting for me at the curb. When I reached it, I stopped and turned to the crowd.

"I didn't want any of this," I began. "That man took someone I cared deeply about, away from me. All I wanted was justice for Joy. I wanted to make him pay. Now it's out of my hands. Hopefully, the system won't let me down this time."

They all started firing off more questions. I got in the cab and told him to floor it. The last thing I needed was to be famous. I wanted to go home. Anonymity sounded fine to me. I didn't do any of the interviews, but I was the lead story on every channel anyway. There was footage of me in Miami. There was more from Galveston, both at the marina, and outside the jail. I was forgiven for violating my probation. Florida was calling me home.

Back to Florida

I wanted to take my time on the return trip. I thought I'd do a little sight-seeing. I had a little money left. The problem was, I was recognized everywhere I stopped. For almost a week, I saw myself on TV. I even saw myself on the cover of a magazine in the grocery store checkout aisle. It freaked me out. I'd lived a life of quiet obscurity, hiding in the shadows. I'd purposely removed myself from the mainstream of society. Now, I was a minor celebrity. I didn't like it much.

As I cruised off the coast of Louisiana, I had to laugh at the situation. If only they knew how I'd stayed alive over the past several years. If only they knew how close I'd come to putting a bullet in Joe's head. How close did I come? I have to admit, I came pretty damn close. For a few seconds, I thought I'd do it. No angel appeared to tell me not to do it. The safety was off.

My finger was on the trigger. The barrel was touching his head. Something stopped me. I didn't cross that line.

The way things turned out, it was a good thing I didn't. There had been a detective watching the boat the whole time. I wouldn't have been a hero if I'd have shot him. I'd have been a murderer. I'd made plenty of bad decisions in my life. This time, I'd done the right thing. Wonders never cease. *There's hope for you yet, Breeze.*

I turned my attention to the future. I had some more decisions to make. The money wouldn't last forever. Joy and I had stashed away thirty grand, after our expenses. I'd spent it freely traveling to Texas. I'd burned through fuel, eaten out at restaurants, and drank in the bars. *Leap of Faith* would need some attention when I got back. It all added up.

I had to decide exactly where to go, at least initially. I wanted to hide from any attention I might receive. The place to do that was Pelican Bay, but I was reluctant to go there. I had always been my refuge. It was home, but it would seem empty now that Joy was gone. There'd be a lot of memories to deal with. I'd go back there someday. For now, I'd let time pass. I'd let the memories get older. I decided to go to Fort Myers Beach.

As soon as I came under the Matanzas Pass Bridge, I saw that *Another Adventure* was gone. I continued past the mooring field and into the backwater where my friends lived. I set the anchor, and prepared the dinghy to go to shore. As always, One-legged Beth was the first to notice my arrival. She came scooting across the river in her skiff to greet me.

"If it ain't the great vigilante Breeze," she said. "We thought you'd forget about us, now that you're famous."

"I could never forget you, Beth," I said. "And go easy on that famous stuff. I'm not comfortable with all the attention."

"Well, you better get used to it," she said. "Everybody up at the bar knows. When new folks show up, they get told the whole story by the locals. One of our own all over the news."

"I was afraid of that," I said. "How did you make out selling Joy's boat?"

"Easy deal," she said. "I think we should have asked for more. It sold so quickly."

"So all three of you are good for money now?" I asked. "No hassles?"

"Yes, and we owe it all to you, and Joy," she answered. "I found the title aboard. Everything was in order. She owned it free and clear."

"What will you do with your new wealth?" I asked.

"Not much really," she answered. "I'm eating better. Got some new clothes."

"Good for you," I said. "Make it last."

"We need to have a party," she said. "Welcome back, Breeze."

We all met for happy hour at the Upper Deck, next door to the dinghy dock. As soon as I entered the bar, Jennifer ran to me and gave me a big hug.

"I didn't know you were such a badass," she whispered.

"Neither did I," I said. "Can you keep it quiet about all that?"

"No way," she answered. "First beer is on me. Hey everybody, Breeze is here. You all line up to buy him a drink."

I spent the next several hours getting slapped on the back, shaking hands, and drinking free beers. I recognized maybe half the customers. Some had familiar faces, but I didn't know their names. There was a magazine cover, in a picture frame, hanging behind the bar. It was me. I couldn't wait for the next big news event to happen. I'd settle for an earthquake, or a plane crash, anything to make folks forget about a boat bum named Breeze.

It happened soon enough. Bruce Jenner decided that he was now Caitlyn. An NAACP chapter president was discovered not to be black at all. Donald Trump announced that he was running for president. The story of the boat bum who tracked his lovers killer, faded from the public eye.

I spent a few days tending to maintenance items. I walked to the NAPA store for oil and filters for *Miss Leap*. I did my duty in the bilge, tightening and lubricating. I inspected thru-hulls and checked fluid levels. I made sure all the pumps were in working order. I loaded up on groceries, beer and rum. I filled the water tanks and the fuel tanks. I was preparing to travel, but to where?

I found myself in a familiar situation. What do I do next? Where is my life going? Although I was technically still on probation, I wasn't wanted by the law. I'd be able to travel freely when it was over. I could get a real job, settle down someplace. I wasn't ready to look for another woman, but there was a real good one back in Punta Gorda. I didn't know what to do, or where to go. I looked for answers in a bottle of rum.

The rum brought out the pirate in me, as it was prone to do. I remembered the offer from Bald Mark. I had some questions for him, so I made the call.

"It's Breeze," I said into the phone. "Can we talk?"

"Breeze, you are one slick son-of-a-bitch," he said. "Is there anything you can't do?"

"Lately, I can't seem to remain anonymous," I said. "If you can help me with that, I'd be more apt to consider your original offer."

"My boat is being hauled out tomorrow," he said. "I go away next week. Put that old boat of yours in my slip. I'll put the word out. No one will bother you there. The rent will be taken care of."

"That's mighty generous," I said.

"I'll expect you to earn it," he said. "You do this for a year, and you'll be set financially."

"Understood," I said. "I'll be there in four or five days."

"You'll need a couple guys," he added. "And I'll buy another fast boat."

So there I was, on my way to the Keys to be a coke runner. That would certainly erase the picture of me as a gallant justice warrior. I'd be hiding out in a secluded marina where no one knew me. I'd be sneaking out at night to pick up bundles of blow. I had a week to get there. I needed to talk to Tiki Terry. I also thought I'd hit Key West on the way.

I went to see Diver Dan and Robin. I sold them on the idea. I talked them into joining my drug running crew with the promise of ridiculous amounts of money. I'd be getting fifty grand a month. I could afford to pay them ten grand each. In twelve months' time I'd have enough cash to live a very long time. My friends would each have over a hundred grand. None of us could turn down this opportunity.

It was a classic case for me. I knew it was wrong, but I was going to do it anyway. I saw the risk as minimal. Bald Mark had police protection down there in the Keys. He would have never had a problem if one of his men hadn't tried to kill me. He'd never actually been caught running the goods. The heat would be off with him in jail. No one but the buyers and the sellers would know what was happening in his absence. I had two good men as crew. What could go wrong?

Key West

There was one place in the country where I could roam about freely without being hassled. I was about to spend a year in seclusion, so I guess I just wanted to let loose a little. Key West was the perfect place to do that. I was short on time, so I ran straight through the night instead of hopping down the coast.

Somewhere off Marco Island, my speed slowed a full knot. The seas were calm. Gauges were within proper operating range. I pulled back on the throttle and shifted into neutral. I went below to check the bilge. It was dry. I was standing on the aft deck when I saw it. A float from a crab trap was bobbing behind the swim platform. I'd hooked it in the darkness. I used a boat hook to snag the line and pulled it in. Half a dozen blue crabs skittered about inside the trap. The crabs went into a bucket. I covered them with a towel and dumped some ice on top. They'd make a nice snack later. The night was black for lack of a moon. If I dove under, I wouldn't be able to see a thing. Instead, I fashioned a knife onto the boat hook. I got down prone on the platform, and reached as far as I could along the line. I sawed it apart.

I put the engine in gear and tried to feel for any odd vibrations. I worked the rudder back and forth. Whatever line remained on the running gear, it didn't seem to be interfering with normal operation. I decided to continue on. I'd dive in the morning. After that short delay, the rest of the crossing was uneventful.

Normally, I liked to anchor near the southwest corner of Fleming Key. It was covered up with boats though. I saw my old friends Jamie and Char tied to a private mooring. I gave them a slow pass and told them I'd get up with them later. I knew from experience that the locals further north on this side of Fleming didn't like newcomers, so I slowly made my way over to Wisteria Island. Well, it used to be called that. The Key West Chamber of Commerce had renamed it, Christmas Tree Island. Tank Island had been partially developed and renamed, Sunset Key. This particular anchorage was populated with run-down vessels and derelicts. Bottom holding was suspect. Assorted characters, vagabonds and pirates roamed between boats. I wouldn't stay here long.

As I was setting the anchor, I heard a dog barking non-stop from a nearby sailboat. The barking continued as I went below for a beer. Two hours later, it was still barking. I got my binoculars to check it out. There was a dinghy tied to the stern, which normally meant someone was aboard. I saw no signs of life, other than the dog. It was obviously in distress. I listened to it howl and carry on for another hour. Finally, I couldn't take it anymore.

I got in my own dinghy and motored over to see what I could see. The dog looked like a pit bull mix, which made me nervous. I hovered a few yards off the port side of the boat to study him. He looked upset, not mean. He would come to the rail and whine, before running to the open companionway to bark. Back and forth he went, whimpering to me, barking at the companionway. I tied off and climbed aboard. The dog didn't attack me. My senses were attacked immediately with two distinct stimuli. A human hand lay on deck. The smell of a decaying corpse hung over the cockpit.

I took two steps to peer down below. The dog stopped his barking. The dead guy was missing a hand. An empty syringe sat on the floor next to his body. *Welcome to Key Weird, Breeze.* The dog and I looked at each other, then back at the body. I tried not to think about the dog chewing on his owner's flesh. He must be starving to death. The body was not freshly dead.

The poor animal probably hadn't eaten or had any water for days.

There were jerry jugs for water tied to the starboard lifelines. I found a bucket and poured a gallon of water in it. My new dog friend drank like his throat was on fire. I took a look around the anchorage. An old guy with a big white beard watched us from the deck of his boat. The authorities needed to be notified, but I was not the man to do it. The last thing I needed was to be in the news again. I loaded the dog into my dinghy and took him over to the bearded man.

"Glad somebody got him to stop barking," he said. "He don't usually do that, but he's been at it for days."

"His owner is dead," I said. "I need you to call somebody, cops or Coast Guard."

"Ain't that a kick in the ass," he said. "Seemed like a decent fellow."

"Can you take the dog for the time being?" I asked. "I can't get caught up in this."

"Put him up here," he answered. "I'll make the call. You can run along. Don't need to know why you can't be involved."

"I appreciate it," I said.

"Same shit, different day," he said. "Welcome to Key West."

After that experience, I needed a beer. I went straight to *Bay Dreamer* to see my friends. We all rode in for happy hour at the

Tower Bar atop Turtle Kraal's. Jamie is a man who doesn't watch the TV news, listen to the radio, or surf the internet. He listened to old Jimmy Buffet tunes over his boat speakers all day and all night. He was proud of his total lack of knowledge on current events. All news was bad news in his opinion. I couldn't really disagree. He knew nothing about my recent adventure in Texas, which was fine by me. He was the perfect drinking companion for that moment. I didn't even mention finding the dead guy. We talked about boat problems and mutual friends over oysters and beer. I put the dismembered hand out of my mind. Afterwards, we saw that a few boats had left the Fleming anchorage. I relocated that night.

The next day, I ventured downtown to Duval Street on my own. I listened to music at the Hog's Breath. I had a few beers at Captain Tony's. I skipped Sloppy Joe's because it was too crowded. I had a few at Willy Tee's. I made my way over to Kelly's. I ended up at the Green Turtle. The band was decent. The girls were pretty, and I was feeling nice and loose. I stepped outside to smoke a cigar and noticed that the wind had kicked up something fierce.

It would be a rough ride back to the boat. I sobered up slightly during the walk to the dinghy dock. When I arrived, a bunch of local live-a-boards were just milling around. An old salt sat on the dock with his bare feet hanging over. His tanned leather face told tales of a life on the water.

"What's up?" I asked the old-timer.

"Waves too big," he answered. "Can't get out there."

The rest of the locals agreed. They discussed sleeping options for the night. Some would take their chances sleeping there, under the docks, until the cops rousted them. Others looked for bushes to bed down in. I was not sleeping under a dock, or in the bushes. I needed to get back to my boat. We all watched as one brave soul got in his dinghy. He was going to take a chance. The rest of them talked of those who had died trying this same stunt. Every year, one or two people failed to make the treacherous trip in seas like these. I climbed the steps to the public restrooms to get a view of the harbor. The waves were way too big for a dinghy to traverse. I watched the guy clear the seawall and enter rough water. He went up and over a few waves, coming perilously close to flipping over backwards. Then he turned around. He came back into the harbor shaking his head. The onlookers lost all hope. If he couldn't make it, neither could they.

There I stood. I was alone on the docks of Key West Bight, facing the prospect of sleeping with the bums in the bushes. Why hadn't I gone straight to Tavernier? I walked over next to the Raw Bar trying to figure out what to do. I saw a guy with a small, odd-looking boat over at the fuel dock. He appeared to be getting ready to go out into the harbor. I walked over to find out. His boat was an old skiff, about fourteen feet long. He had not one, not two, but three outboards clamped to the transom. He told me that one didn't run. One ran, but needed some work. The center one was running fine. He had a half-submerged dinghy tied off to the back of his skiff. He told me he found it floating free and rescued it. The skiff itself was full of junk.

"You going out there, in that?" I asked.

"Sure am," he replied. "I'll be fine. I'll just go slow and easy. This boat will make it."

"I'll pay you to take me and my dinghy back out to my boat," I offered.

"No problem," he said. "The name's Bruce."

"Breeze," I said, offering my hand.

I was about to discover that Bruce was the craziest fool of all the crazy fools in Key West. There are a lot of crazy people in that town. I had put my life in the hands of their king.

It started out normal enough. We slogged along about one knot. The Coast Guard Station and a rock wall were on our starboard side. The bigger waves would push us backward, but the little boat was sturdy. We'd make some progress between waves. We'd gain twenty yards, before being pushed back five yards. At the end of the rock wall, two channels intersected. The water here was rough in calms winds. Darkness had fallen before we made the intersection. It was a washing machine on steroids. The colliding currents pushed the waves up to impossible angles. We were spun sideways and almost capsized. Crazy Bruce gunned the throttle and regained control. He said we were going to be okay, which was reassuring. Then he started howling at the moon. This was not reassuring. He was like George Clooney in *The Perfect Storm*.

"Is that all you got?" he yelled at the waves. "I am Captain Bruce. You can't kill me motherfucker."

I hunkered down on the deck of the little skiff and held on tight. We were almost out of the cross-current. The waves were now breaking over the bow, drenching us both. Assorted junk floated around our ankles. Just as we reached the relative calm of the main harbor, Bruce poked me in the back and yelled over the sound of the wind.

"That sailboat is dragging anchor," he said, pointing at a nearby vessel. "I'm supposed to be keeping an eye on it for my buddy."

"What the hell can we do?" I asked.

"We gotta save it," he answered. "It'll bust up on the rocks."

I shook my head no as he turned towards the drifting boat. I was at his mercy. I should have slept in the bushes. We came up behind it. Just as we approached, as large wave lifted us. We came down the other side fast, and rammed the sailboat. The shock of the impact threw me forward. I was on my hands and knees when we rammed it again.

"What the hell are you doing?" I screamed.

"Trying to stop her momentum, let the anchor grab," he answered.

"You're going to crack us up," I yelled.

"Can you climb aboard her?" he asked.

"No, I'm not climbing up there," I said. "I've been drinking all day. I'm wearing flip flops, and it's too damn rough."

"Take the tiller," he said. "I'll climb over."

Things were happening too fast for me to protest. Crazy Bruce was moving forward and no one was at the tiller. I scrambled on my hands and knees to the rear. Bruce yelled for me to throttle up, get us closer. That's when the motor quit. We had wrapped a lobster trap line in the prop. It had stopped the outboard cold. We bobbed about violently, anchored by the weight of the trap. The two dinghies we had in tow bounced off the skiff and added to the confusion.

"There's a knife on here somewhere," yelled Bruce.

I rummaged through the junk until I found a rusty bait knife. Bruce took it and started hacking at the line. When it broke, we started drifting towards the rocks at the Coast Guard Station.

The prop was still fouled with line, but we were floating free. Bruce continued slashing at rope and cussing the Gods.

"I'll kill me a lobsterman," he screamed. "I'll cut these frigging dinghies loose too."

"The rocks, man," I said. "We're getting close to the rocks."

We were thirty yards from the jagged wall of the Coast Guard Station when he quit trying to cut the prop free. He switched the fuel line over to another outboard and starting pulling the starter rope. With each pull he screamed up at the night sky. He cursed God and Poseidon. He cursed the universe in general.

"Fuck you all," he screamed. "You can't kill me."

"The rocks!" I warned.

"I fucking see the fucking rocks, motherfucker," he yelled back.

Fifteen yards separated us from certain death when the little motor fired up. Crazy Bruce laughed maniacally as we turned away from the rocks. I whispered thanks to Jesus and apologies to Poseidon. Sleeping in the bushes wasn't such a bad idea after all. Again, we crossed the colliding currents, barely making headway. Just as we cleared the worst of it, the little motor quit. Bruce resumed screaming. He yanked the cord over and over, yelling and cussing. We drifted back towards the rocks a second time.

It sputtered to life and I said another prayer. Bruce grabbed my shoulder and scared the crap out of me.

"We're not going to make it on this motor," he said. "We need to clear the prop on the good motor somehow."

It was impossible to think clearly under the circumstances. The howling of the wind and the crashing of the waves was driving me mad. We rose and fell as each new wave crested. The motor was coughing and spitting like it was ill. He was right. It wouldn't last long.

"Try to make it to the closest boat," I said. "I'll hold on to it while you clear the prop."

We made slow progress towards a powerboat anchored just outside the channel. I could almost reach it when the motor died once again. The skiff was quickly pushed back in the wind and waves. The screams that came out of Bruce were neither human nor animal. He was a raging demon from hell. He stood up and put his hands to the sky and let out a long, primordial scream.

"The knife, Bruce," I said. "Clear the prop."

He leaned out over the transom and started hacking at the rope. I couldn't decide if it would be good or bad if he fell over. My dinghy drifted in to us and he accidentally cut the line holding it to the skiff. I grabbed the dinghy and pulled in what was left of the line. I worked to retie it as Bruce sawed away.

He let out a giggle of delight as the last bit of it came free. He switched the fuel line back to the good motor and fired it up. He throttled up and away we went for a third time.

I soon realized that he intended to continue his rescue effort of his buddy's sailboat. I'd had enough. Bruce was a Wildman. He was much bigger than me, obviously insane, and not someone I'd normally stand up to. But I couldn't take it any longer. I grabbed him by his collar with both hands. I looked him dead in the eye. I pulled his face close to mine.

"You take me to my boat right now, mother fucker," I said sternly. "You get me to my boat and you can do any damn fool thing you want. My boat, right now."

"Okay," he said. "I understand. Don't worry. We're gonna make it."

We traveled the rest of the way in silence. I was cold, wet, and miserable. Every minute of the way had been life threatening, and it wasn't over yet. I could see *Miss Leap* bucking up and down like a frightened horse. Her anchor was still holding. Other boats in the neighborhood were not so lucky.

Bruce brought us up behind her slowly. She was rising and falling five feet at a time. We were also rising and falling. Two moving platforms danced a dangerous dance. I stood on the bow of the skiff trying to time the waves. I started to jump and Bruce screamed, "Not now!" I held his bow line and concentrated on the movement of the boats. He screamed again, "Now!" I leapt across onto the swim platform, grabbing at the transom. The platform went below the waves and I lost my footing, but held on with my hands. I lunged through the transom door and into the aft cockpit, still holding his bow line.

"Get my dinghy up here," I yelled to Bruce.

"You need to take both of them," he yelled back. "I'm going after my buddy's boat."

"Whatever," I responded. "Tie them both off and go. Good luck."

He handed me the line to my dinghy and I tied it off. We got the swamped dinghy tied off on the other side. I handed him forty bucks before he left. He briefly objected, but took the money. Then he motored off into the waves to tilt at windmills, or slay dragons, or sink and die. I entered my salon in search of rum. My hands were shaking as I twisted the cap. I took a long slug straight from the bottle. The trembling slowed. I was on my boat and I was alive. It wasn't the wind and waves that I had survived. I had survived Crazy Bruce. Once again, I questioned why I ever came to Key West.

Bruce survived the night. The next day he returned to take possession of the other dinghy, I couldn't decide if I was happy or not, that he had made it. I would later be warned to never, under any circumstances, deal with Crazy Bruce. He was a pirate and a thief. The tales of his crazy exploits were shared throughout the boating community. If only I had known.

My Own Cartel

I met up with Tiki Terry, Diver Dan, and Robin at Dockside in Boot Key Harbor. I had anchored in the center of the harbor, just off the main channel. Dan and Robin were anchored in Sister Creek. I made the introductions over cold beers. We used the meeting as a team building session. No specifics of what we were about to do were mentioned. We'd do that in private.

Terry was making arrangements for my crew to store their boats near Tavernier. I had Bald Mark's slip waiting for me. We debated what type of fast boat to buy. I did not want a loud Cigarette or Donzi. I pushed the argument that an offshore center console with triple outboards would be less conspicuous and quieter than the typical go-fast beast. I convinced the others. Terry set out to do a little research on various makes. We wanted it fast, just as fast as Mark's old boats.

Bald Mark was set to appear in court, and eventually the custody of Florida's correctional system in two days. I wanted to see him before he left. I was about to assume half of his illegal operation. In return, I've have a place to lie low, out of the public eye. I'd also make a crap load of cash.

I pulled into his slip late the next day. He was at his usual table in the tiki bar.
"Nothing like waiting for the last minute," he said in greeting.
"I've rested and recreated," I said. "Now I'm ready to rock."
"Your crew is ready too?" he asked.
"My guys are in Marathon," I answered. "Terry is getting them something closer."
"Terry is a sharp guy," he said. "He and I have come to an understanding. Do what he says, he'll be getting directions from me. Now you and I need to come to a similar understanding."
"You trust me," I began. "But if I screw up, or cross you in any way, I'm a goner."
"That's pretty much the gist of it," he said. "I'm putting the past behind us. I've learned that you get shit done. I've observed some sort of code you follow. You saved that Cuban

girl. You avenged that chick that got shot in Miami. I think you're straight up. Don't disappoint me."

"I've got no reason to," I said. "I'm here to make money for me and my friends. I don't care about the rest of it."

"Terry will take care of the rest of it," he said.

"Enjoy your vacation," I offered.

"I'll be back in a year, or less," he said. "Keep the roof on for me."

He got up and walked out. Before leaving, he used his black eyes to look deep into my soul. It gave me a chill. I was on his good side now. I didn't ever want to be on his bad side. I walked back to my boat, pondering the latest turn my life had taken.

Over the next few days, our little team went over charts to determine likely locations offshore to pick up our loads. We took delivery of our new chase boat. Robin would run it. He'd be armed with my shotgun. Dan would be with me on Leap of Faith. He would carry a pistol. Everyone understood their roles.

Our first test seemed like an easy one. We'd meet the same shrimper I had taken delivery from before. The Dragonfly would slow troll towards the Dry Tortugas. We'd intercept off the Marquesas and transfer the goods. It went off without a hitch. After we stowed the coke below, we ran all night, back to Tavernier. I brought the drug shipment right into the marina.

Terry took it from there. We met later to get our cut. I got fifty grand. I gave Dan and Robin each ten grand out of my share. We celebrated by getting rip-roaring drunk aboard *Leap of Faith*. When I woke up, I found Robin asleep on the settee. Dan was passed out in a deck chair.

On the next trip, we took a mooring ball off Sombrero Key. We used the chase boat to run further offshore to meet a shrimper. We spent the night out there on the ball. We did a little snorkeling in the morning before returning to home base. We collected our cash and took a few weeks off. It was all so easy. We had no problems. I hadn't been nervous at all. It wasn't rocket science, after all. It was just a nighttime boat ride. All we did was transfer freight.

That all changed on our third run. We were hovering off Boca Grande Key at midnight, when we were approached by another boat. We couldn't see it at first, but we could hear it. It came directly alongside my trawler. It was painted a flat black. The motors were black, with no decals. The chrome trim had been covered in black. Dan hit it with a spotlight. A driver and two armed men were aboard. They wore all black clothes and masks.

It immediately became clear that their intentions were not good. There was no indication that this was law enforcement. I called out for them to identify themselves. We'd done nothing illegal yet. We hadn't met the shrimper.

"We are taking your vessel," said the driver of the black boat. "We will make the rendezvous, and take custody of the cargo. If you cooperate you won't be harmed. We will return your boat."

I heard the shotgun blast and saw the driver go down. Dan started firing from the bridge. One of the other men on the black boat sprayed us with bullets. The shotgun blasted off again and he went down. The third man was wounded, and trying to reload. Dan reloaded first and pumped five shots into his center mass. I heard Robin rack the slide on the shotgun. A spent shell tinkled on the deck of our chase boat.

"Holly fuck," yelled Robin. "I didn't have a choice, Breeze."

"I don't know what that was all about," I said. "Good shooting, both of you. Let's get out of here. We've got a shrimp boat to meet."

We were only a few minutes late arriving at the shrimper's location. We slowed to a crawl and rafted together briefly. The packages were transferred quickly. Robin was looking all around in every direction, keeping watch over us. Dan was muttering something under his breath that sounded like "frigging drugs." No more bad guys appeared. I made an executive decision not to return to the marina. Instead I chose

Stock Island, like I'd done on my first trip for Bald Mark. I called Terry to tell him what happened and where we were. He came for the coke, and took it the rest of the way by land.

The reality of what business we were in, settled on all of us. There were three dead men floating near Boca Grande Key. Someone knew about our operation. Maybe it was one of the dead guys, but somehow I doubted it. What I really wanted to do was take what I'd made so far and run. That's what I'd always done, but there was Bald Mark to consider. I'd promised him that his coke would continue to flow in. Terry promised him that it would continue to flow out. We weren't getting paid so richly for joyrides. It was a mean and dirty business.

I asked Diver Dan and Robin how they felt about it. There would be no hard feelings if they decided to quit.

"I never shot a man in my life," said Robin. "I never thought I would, but it was them or us."

"You did what had to be done," said Dan. "If you're going to run with devils, you got to be a devil yourself."

"You ever shot a man, Dan?" asked Robin.

"Ain't something to be proud of," Dan answered.

"What about you, Breeze?"

"I shot a man with bird shot up in Pelican Bay," I said. "That was after he put a hundred bullets into this boat. If it was buckshot or a slug he'd be dead. I almost shot that guy in Texas, but I couldn't bring myself to do it."

"I'd prefer not to have to shoot people," said Robin.

"You just might have to," Dan snorted. "If we're gonna ride this out, it will happen again. Frigging drugs always come to shooting."

"It's up to you two," I said. "I'm staying, but you don't have to."

They were both quiet for a long time. Neither of them had ever had much in life. They barely existed financially. They were the people that didn't count in this world. They were off the grid, anonymous. They scraped by on their wits and their will. I had no idea what they would decide. Finally, Dan spoke.

"We signed on for a tour of duty," he said. "I plan to honor my obligation. I knew all along it wouldn't be all fun and games."

"I'm in too," said Robin. "The money is just too much for me to walk away."

"All right," I said. "We need to toughen up. We need more firepower. We need to find out who tried to bust up our operation. We need to do all that before we ride again."

We all drank until we couldn't speak. We littered the deck with empty beer cans and rum bottles. We drowned the regret of dead men in alcohol.

Terry questioned all his contacts for information on the attempted act of piracy. He got permission from Bald Mark to increase our armaments. He worked his network, trying to find out who was trying to take us down. I worked out new scenarios for the pickups. We made a few false runs at night, trying to detect anyone following us or watching us too closely. We saw nothing out of the ordinary, but I wasn't taking chances.

On our next run, we left two days early. We moved the boat into Newfound Harbor for the night. We saw nothing. We continued on to Key West the next day. No followers were spotted. We scheduled our meeting with the shrimper up above the Northwest Channel, in the Gulf of Mexico. The captain complained about the extra mileage. We handed him two cases of beer and a bottle of rum for his troubles. He shut up.

We brought our cargo back through Florida Bay, to Islamorada. Robin and Dan loaded up the chase boat with fishing gear and pretended to be fishermen. They ran the coke out into Hawk Channel and up to Tavernier in broad daylight. They were not detected by law enforcement, or bad guys. The deal was done and we got paid once again.

During our downtime, the source of our earlier trouble was discovered. Bald Mark's former right-hand man, Enrique, had talked too much from his jail cell. Some resourceful fellow inmate had gotten too much information about how Bald Mark ran his operation. Word made its way to the outside. I felt no remorse when I learned of Enrique's death. He was found with his throat slit. I thought to myself, bad things happen to bad people. What about me? Was I a bad person now? I was helping to supply the entire Florida Keys, and parts of Miami, with cocaine. Would I meet a fate similar to Enrique? What about my friends? Had I drug them into something horrible, or had they come of their own free will?

This sort of contemplation always hurt my head. Right is right, and wrong is wrong. I knew the difference. What the hell was I doing? The line had been stretched when Joy and I fleeced those men on the east coast. It had been broken all to hell when I agreed to work for Bald Mark. I couldn't get out. Mark would have me killed, or I'd be running and hiding forever. I was stuck. I had to do my job, finish out my term. I'd quit as soon as he got out of jail.

I couldn't be sure if we'd be attacked or hijacked by the people who knew our business again. I changed up our methods once again. We laid up *Leap of Faith* off Crocker Reef, due south of Tavernier. Dan and Robin ran south into the Atlantic Ocean to meet the shrimp boats outside territorial limits. They brought the goods back to me and we stashed them in the hold. We'd sit and fish, snorkel, and drink beer for a while. We headed back into the marina, and got paid. It worked so well, we did it three times. The third time was once too many.

As we transferred the coke bundles from the chase boat onto my trawler, Dan spotted another boat approaching. He put the binoculars on it, and said it looked like the law. We quickly put the coke back on the faster boat and Robin took off like a rocket. We watched him fade from sight as he hit over 80 miles per hour on the smooth sea. It was several minutes later when the DEA boat pulled alongside.

"What was your buddies hurry?" asked the agent.

"He smoked a joint and was afraid you'd bust him," I answered.

"We don't give a shit about that," he said. "We're looking for smugglers."

"We've just been fishing and drinking a few beers," I said. "You're welcome to come aboard."

"Can't even go fishing these days without some alphabet agency harassing you," huffed Dan.

The officer came aboard, and made a cursory inspection of the boat. He was not very thorough. Before he left, he mentioned casually that he'd radioed a chopper on our buddy.

"Have a nice day," he said, before motoring away.

Dan reached for his phone to warn Robin. The chase boat had rocketed south without seeing any helicopters. Robin had wedged the boat into some mangroves near the Saddlebunch Keys. He could hear the traffic on US 1 from where he hid. He was afraid a chopper would spot him. We were afraid we'd lose the whole load of coke if that happened. We listened to Robin complain about the mosquitoes and lack of drinking water for a few minutes. No one was really sure what we should do next. If we moved *Leap of Faith*, the DEA would notice. If Robin sat put, they might see him eventually.

I instructed Robin to set out on foot and try to find a way to the road. I called Tiki Terry and told him about our predicament. Then we waited. Robin called back with some news. He had made it to US 1. There was a spot for a car or truck to pull over. I listened to the description carefully, so I could relay it to Terry. It took several hours, but the coke was rescued from the mangroves and Robin was rescued from the mosquitoes. He could proceed in the chase boat without fear. They might see him and stop him, but he was drug free now. Diver Dan and I continued fishing and drinking beer. Robin cruised into Boot Key Harbor and had some beers at Dockside. We all met up back in Tavernier the following day.

We'd had a run-in with pirates hoping to hijack our load. Now we'd had a run-in with the law. It was time to lay low for a while. Terry wasn't pleased with this latest development. Bald Mark sent a message to me. Get my head out of my ass and get serious about security. There was a ton of tension in the air. I needed a vacation. This drug-running game was serious business, no fun at all. I decided to leave the Keys, and hide out in Pelican Bay until it was time to make another run. I needed a little communion with Mother Ocean. I wanted to hear the breath of dolphins again. Dan and Robin worried about Beth back in Fort Myers Beach. We spent the next day readying our vessels. We all traveled together back up the west coast until we reached the Matanzas Pass. I veered off and continued through San Carlos Bay and north for Cayo Costa.

I was going home.

Self-Reflection

It was the same every time. Entering Pelican Bay always helped to release whatever burden I was bearing. My spirits lifted. My soul got a little lighter. This place made me feel safe. Being here made me happy.

I secured the anchor and did my maintenance checks. All was well with *Miss Leap*. She'd been as steadfast and sturdy as ever. I did a quick walk-around and noticed some teak that would soon need a new coat of varnish. I made a mental list of other chores that I could take care of while I was here. Then I just sat down to think. There was no sound at first. The quiet was deafening. Slowly, my ear picked up the sounds around me. I heard the ospreys chirping on the island. Pelicans splashed, diving for bait. A mother dolphin with her baby alongside rose to breath. Small wavelets lapped at the hull. I let myself decompress. I pushed recent events from my conscious mind.

An hour passed. I just sat there, fixated on nature. Finally, I went inside for a beer. I spotted the little canister with what was left of Laura's ashes. It was in a basket on the console. I picked it up and took it with me to the aft deck. I hadn't done that in a long time, but the guilt was less than ever. Time was healing me. Laura's death was the event that triggered everything. It was how I ended up here now. It was why I had this boat. Losing her had sent me on a path that had continually spiraled downward. I'd climbed up from the depths of despair a time or two. Each time, I'd fallen to new lows.

Growing dope and selling it on my own had seemed innocent enough. That had grown into smuggling pounds of weed into the Keys every month. Scamming unfaithful husbands out of money hadn't seemed so bad at first. That had resulted in Joy's death. I had justified signing up with Bald Mark that first time. I needed the money to cross an ocean. I had to find Andi, and my half-million dollars. I spent almost every dime of it staying out of jail. Now I was a full-time coke smuggler. Could I get any lower?

"I'm sorry, Laura," I said. "I know you can't be proud of me now, but I'll figure something out. I always do. It'll work out."

She didn't answer. The canister just sat there, all banged up and taped over. Her ashes had been through a lot. I'd carried them halfway around the world and back, twice. They'd survived a gun battle. They'd survived other women aboard our boat. Laura's ashes had comforted me when things were bleak. They were my last connection to the life I'd left behind. It seemed so long ago.

I needed to forge a path forward. I'd been bouncing around from one crisis to the next. I was surviving, but it wasn't enough anymore. This life had nearly starved me, and nearly landed me in jail. My luck was due to run out sooner or later. The sun and the salt had hardened me. There were people in my life, but no one in my heart. I had friends, but it seemed so shallow. I was a hollow man. The realization stung me. I was happy and loving once. I cared. Now I didn't care so much. I only thought of the next score, or the next port. I only cared about staying out of prison.

I'd come close with Andi. She was the perfect woman who came into my life at the perfect time, but I'd lost her. I never truly let her in to my heart and soul. I'd held her at arm's length. She played second fiddle to my boat, and my mission. She dutifully carried out her role. She helped me accomplish my task, and then she left. When I saw her again in Luperon, I had Yolanda with me, and a new mission. Andi finished second yet again. Could I return to her? Would she even have me, at this point? Is that what I wanted? At the end of the year, I'd have enough money to make it all happen. I'd always toyed with running to the islands and living a life of leisure with a beautiful woman. I shelved this train of thought for later consideration.

I wondered what had become of Yolanda. I was forced to smuggle her out of Cuba, to save my own ass. Then I became fond of her, and her of me. I promised her a new life in America, and I delivered on that promise. It just didn't include me. I dropped her off with distant relatives in Baltimore, and fled for my life. I'd probably never see her again. Then I started considering that possibility. I'd be free from the law soon. I could go to her. Would she want me? Is that what I wanted? I shelved that train of thought for future consideration too.

Then there was Joy. The thought of her brought a twinge of grief. I'd settled my score with her killer. I hadn't really come to grips with losing her. I'd simply shoved my feelings deep down inside and tried hard not to think about her. I was out there all alone, thinking about the women in my life, so I let myself think of Joy. I pictured her in my mind as a smiling pixie, dancing through life without a care. I smiled as I remembered our time together right here in this bay. We had been buddies. We had been friends with benefits. We hadn't given our hearts to one another completely. There was always a slight separation. We were two broken souls sharing a life. I hoped I'd been as good for her as she had been for me. Now she was gone. I couldn't do a damn thing about that. There was no future to consider for her and me.

I couldn't help but feel grateful for all those good women who'd graced my life. They were all gone now, but I'd been blessed. I'd run them away, or they'd died on me, but each held a special place in my heart. I smiled again, picturing each at their best. I remembered all the good qualities of each of them. I'd been so in love with Laura. Her gift was to allow me to truly and fully give myself over to love. Andi's beauty was a gift in itself. Yolanda's quiet dignity and solid heart helped me to see the good in people. She saw the good in me, even when I didn't.

It was amazing really. A boat bum like me with a trail of fantastic women left behind. What did they see in me? How had I ever attracted them in the first place? It was a mystery to me. Then I remembered Taylor. How had I forgotten? I pictured her cute figure with her shapely legs under those short skirts. I saw her auburn hair cascading down on her shoulders, curving around those sexy glasses. She was a hot school teacher or naughty librarian. She was also brilliant. She too had shown interest in me, even though she knew my crimes. I guessed I had something going for me. I'd been alone a lot in my life, but there had been those women. Fine women had shown up at just the right times. I shouldn't mourn that. I'd been damn fortunate.

I decided that all this reflection called for a toast. The seal on a new bottle of rum was broken. I raised a shot glass and made a toast for all of them.

"To Laura," I said aloud. "Who gave me love, and taught me that love was real."

I downed a shot of rum, and poured another.

"To Andi," I said. "Who saved me from myself and rescued me from despair."

I downed another shot, and poured another.

"To Yolanda," I said. "Who taught me to appreciate goodness. May you never lose your dignity."

Another shot was slugged down. I refilled the glass.

"To Joy," I said. "Who taught me to be a friend, and to appreciate friends. I'm so sorry."

Another shot. Another refill.

"To Taylor," I said. "Who made me realize I have something to offer, and that I am worthy. May we meet again."

Five quick shots made me light headed. I sat down in the chair, put my feet up on the transom, and fell sound asleep. My dreams were a slideshow of those women. I ached in my heart for them all. The last shot was of Taylor. It lingered there. She wasn't gone. She was still there. She was alive and within reach. I woke up thinking about her.

I spent the whole day thinking about her. I considered making the twenty mile run to Punta Gorda and giving her a call. I'd have to explain my absence over the past six months. I'd have a lot of questions to answer about what I'd been doing. I decided against it, for now. I needed to focus on Bald Mark's operation. I needed to protect my friends, and myself. I'd finish it out. Then I'd return and call Taylor.

I turned my attention to my boat. I spent a week sanding and applying new varnish where needed. I walked on the beach. I swam in the Gulf. I listened to the breath of dolphins. I drank coffee as the sun rose. I drank beer as it set. I prepared myself mentally and physically to go back to the Keys and bring in the coke. I'd get it done. I'd get paid. I'd leave when it was done.

I had a new enthusiasm. Soon I'd be free of my obligation to Bald Mark. Soon I'd be free of my legal troubles. I was about to have an opportunity to start all over again. I could remake my life in any way I chose. Pelican Bay had cured me again. I felt good. I was ready to get this over with. I was ready to move on in life.

Smuggling Trouble

I met up with Diver Dan and Robin in Fort Myers Beach. They told me of the intervention they had with One-legged Beth. She'd used some of the money we left her, to buy some coke of her own. The three of us had hauled about a ton of the stuff, and never touched it. Meanwhile, Beth was snorting enough for all four of us while we were gone. They had locked her up on Dan's boat to dry her out. She bitched and moaned for a few days, but eventually she came around.

Now she was thankful for the care they had given her. I was thankful that we had taken a break and returned from the Keys. Unchecked, she would have eventually gone broke, or died. I didn't want to take her with us, though. We decided instead, to take her money. Robin would send her an allowance weekly.

With that settled, we returned to Tavernier and the coke smuggling business.

We were met with difficulty as soon as we arrived. Terry told us that our Key West distributor couldn't move his product. Someone else had flooded the market with good quality blow and was selling it cheap. It was a classic maneuver for dealers trying to get a foothold in a new territory. When Bald Mark was around, he'd send his five tough hombres down to handle it. A few legs would get broken, or worse, and the trouble would disappear. The three of us were ill-equipped to handle the problem in the same manner. We weren't tough hombres, and we didn't relish the thought of violence.

Tiki Terry and Bald Mark worked the coconut network to get information on the interlopers. We learned that a fishing guide was bringing it in, probably on a flats boat. He returned to Key West from Florida Bay, probably picking it up in the Everglades, or Ten Thousand Islands. We only knew that the dealer was living on a boat anchored in the harbor. We didn't know which boat. There were about five hundred boats anchored off of Key West. I knew that one of those boats belonged to Crazy Bruce. I hoped he wasn't involved. He was a scary dude.

I took *Leap of Faith* down to Key West and took a slip at The Galleon. I got a room overlooking the harbor, with a nice view of all the anchored boats. I set up a telescope on a tripod and surveyed them. Dan and Robin arrived and we set up shifts. We took turns watching the comings and goings of the boaters. I watched a black cowboy with a guitar on his back, yanking on the starter rope of his outboard a dozen times before giving up. Someone else came along and towed him into Key West Bight. I caught Robin using the scope to check out the bikinis on the Fury Charters sunset cruise.

The sun went down but it wasn't full dark yet. Dan spotted a flats boat approaching an anchored sailboat off Christmas Tree Island. A man appeared on deck. Three backpacks were handed up to him, and the smaller boat left. The man took the packages below and disappeared inside his boat. This was probably what we were looking for.

The three of us hustled down to the docks and boarded our chase boat. We idled out of the Bight and slowly made our way across the harbor. Robin cut the motors as we approached and we glided the last twenty yards to the bow of the sailboat. Dan made short work of the anchor rode with a dive knife. We set the sailboat adrift without making a sound. We drifted away towards the west. Robin re-fired the motors before we grounded and we pulled away.

We all watched as the sailboat drifted up onto the shore of Christmas Tree Island. Soon after it heeled over, we saw the man inside come out on deck. We approached him and offered our assistance, which he accepted. Dan and I boarded with a long tow line. Robin positioned the chase boat and the line was heaved across to him. I gave a signal, and braced myself. Dan grabbed the forward rail to hold on. The boat owner didn't see it coming. Robin jammed the throttles forward and yanked us all violently. Our target fell to the deck, and Dan was on him. He felt the cold steel of a pistol on the back of his neck.

I went below to retrieve the backpacks. They were still out in the open, sitting on the salon table. I tossed them over to Robin. I jumped down into the boat with him. Dan gave our victim a good whack on the head with the butt of the gun, before jumping aboard himself. He'd have no product to sell this week. We roared off to the north, before turning east and circling Fleming Key. We came back in by Garrison Bight, before idling back into the Galleon. We cleaned out the room, loaded the boats, and left for points north.

We'd sent a loud message. The rival operation would be on notice that a violation of Bald Mark's territory wouldn't be tolerated. We'd broken no legs. We'd left no dead bodies behind. We thought we'd put a stop to it.

When we made it back to Tavernier, we learned that something similar was going on in Key Largo. This was not good. Bald Mark's absence had emboldened everyone wanting to get in the drug running game. My amigos and I couldn't run all over the Keys smacking them all down. I wasn't sure what to do. Tiki Terry didn't know what to do either. We all agreed that he needed to talk with Bald Mark. We were holding the fort for him, but it was his business.

I didn't like the prospect of violence. I was too close to freedom for this shit. I was afraid Mark would call for an all-out war. He didn't. Instead he reinvented his little corporation. He was graduating from the local markets. We'd bring in the big score. He wanted us to take *Leap of Faith* to South America and load it to the gills with coke. We run it right into Miami. The resulting supply would shock the market. Bald Mark would wait for the other players to come to him to negotiate. He was fearless. I was not. South America?

We were going to Columbia, to be precise. All the arrangements were made. We were mules now, about to carry a ton of cocaine in a slow boat to Florida. We'd be at sea for two weeks, at least. It would be a grueling trip for both crew and vessel. I supervised preparations to my boat. We lined the holds in the bilge with thick plastic. We added fuel bladders to increase our range. We kept busy making sure *Miss Leap* was ship-shape. It would be a long haul for her. It would be a long haul for all of us.

On a break, Diver Dan came to me with his concerns. He had some good ones. The biggest was compensation. We'd be bringing millions worth of product back. His measly ten grand cut was not enough, for the risk involved. Robin was in agreement. Hell, I was in agreement. It was a valid point. I told Tiki Terry that I needed to speak with Bald Mark directly. He set it up. He sent word for Mark to fill out a visitor information form and mail it to us. Visiting hours at the Federal Correctional Institution, in Miami, were only on the weekends. Since I wasn't a family member, I'd need the form to get in. It came in the mail within a few days.

Terry drove me to Miami the following Saturday. He waited while I went in to talk to Mark.

"It ain't my birthday, Breeze," said Mark.

"How you holding up?" I asked.

"Beat's working for a living," he replied. "Great food, comfy accommodations, golf on Sundays. It's almost as nice as living at the marina. The only problem is no beer."

"Not drinking beer is a punishment in itself," I said.

"Terry says you have a problem," he said.

"Yes, we all do," I said. "The normal percentage doesn't calculate favorably with what you've asked us to do. It's outside the scope of our original agreement."

I didn't know if we were being watched or listened to in the meeting room. It was an open lounge with nice furniture, much nicer than what I'd seen during my jail time. I tried to keep my language vague enough to not incriminate us, just in case.

"I'm willing to upgrade the compensation package significantly," he said. "I can't make other arrangements from in here. This trip, with you and your crew, it's got to work."

"I can make it happen," I said. "The guys will be on board, as long as I bring home the bacon."

He picked up a pen from the table, and tore a page out of a magazine. In the margin, he wrote a figure. He slid the torn page over to me. He had offered me two hundred thousand. He had also suggested a split of one hundred thousand for me, and fifty thousand for each of my crew. I looked into his black eyes. He was impossible to read. He slowly shook his head no. I took that to mean I shouldn't ask for more. This was his final offer. I could take it or leave it. If I didn't make the run for him, our relationship would be finished. I knew that wouldn't turn out well for me.

"Accepted," I said.

"Smart man," he replied. "I'll have Terry reimburse you for fuel and expenses. The three of you keep the whole payday."

"Fair enough," I said. "We'll make it happen."

"This will be the end of it, Breeze, if that's what you want. I'll be out of here soon. Do this for me, collect on it, and we can part ways."

"I think I'll do just that," I said. "No offense intended. I've fulfilled my end of the deal."

"There will be no hard feelings," he said. "Good luck to you."

"Good luck to you," I said.

I walked out of there feeling much better. We still had this dangerous trip to make, but I could see the end of my servitude. I'd have more cash than I could carry. I'd be rich, for about the third time. My friends would have plenty of money too. We could get this done, and ride off into the sunset.

To Cartagena

Bald Mark's offer was accepted by Diver Dan and Robin. We loaded up the boat with food, water and beer. The fuel tanks were topped off. Robin made a run to the post office to send One-legged Beth her allowance. We wouldn't be back for a couple of weeks.

We spent our first night at sea anchored near Fort Jefferson, in the Dry Tortugas. We sat on the bridge drinking beer and going over our plans. We were to take four hour shifts at the helm. Each man would have eight hours off duty to rest, drink beer, or whatever. There would be no drinking at the helm, or within four hours of taking your shift. The safety of the vessel was our number one priority. We wanted to be successful with our return cargo, but we wanted to survive first. We were all a little nervous about the trip. I was the only one with any real blue water experience. I was confident in *Leap of Faith*. She was slow but steady. We'd get there and back.

We finished our beers and went to bed, each with visions of dollar signs dancing in our head.

I awoke before daylight to the unmistakable sound of a shotgun being racked. It was Robin. He had all of our weapons laid out in the main salon. A can of gun oil and some rags lay on the floor. He gave me a determined look.

"The guns are all cleaned and ready," he said.

"Can't be too prepared," I said. "But I hope we don't need them this time."

"Why do you think we never heard nothing about those dudes we shot?" he asked.

"Might still be floating out here somewhere," I said. "Who knows?"

"I thought I'd be creeped out about killing a man," he said. "But it hasn't bothered me. It was us or them, Breeze."

"It bothers me some," I admitted. "But this isn't child's play. We all signed up for hazardous duty."

"What are you going to do with all your money?" he asked.

"I'm still working that out," I told him. "I always wanted to just disappear and never come back. Take a pretty woman out to the islands and live like a king forever."

"Sounds nice," he said. "I'm thinking along those same lines myself."

"Just need the right woman to fulfill the dream," I said.

"That's always the thing, isn't it?" he replied.

We both nodded in agreement. He went back to his gun cleaning. I found Diver Dan on the aft deck. He had a big can of Foster's beer in his hand. It was six in the morning.

"I don't go on duty for eight hours," he said.

"It's okay," I replied. "You been thinking about what you're going to do after this is over?"

"I reckon I'll get a new boat," he said. "I'll sell all of my junk, or give it away. I'll make sure Beth has a nice place to live."

"You going to travel?" I asked.

"I guess I could do that if I got a new boat," he answered. "Hadn't really thought about it."

"I want to thank both of you for hanging in with me on this," I said.

"I'll thank you if we make it back home in one piece, with the money," he said. "I'm too old for this shit, Breeze. I'm afraid this is my last adventure."

"We do this right, we can all retire," I told him.

We both nodded in agreement, and he went back to drinking his beer.

The weather was right. The sapphire sky reflected off the blue sea. Winds were forecasted to be light or nonexistent over the coming few days. At seven knots, *Miss Leap* would cover one hundred and sixty-eight nautical miles per day. I took the first shift at the helm while Dan and Robin made breakfast below. The distance seemed impossible. The urge to speed her up was strong, but if I did, we'd run out of fuel. All we could do was chug along at that speed for days on end. Once Fort Jefferson fell out of sight behind us, there was nothing to see but a thousand miles of deep blue.

Robin took over four hours later. I told him to relax and follow the course I had plotted on the GPS. Keep her at seven knots. He did fine. Dan took over for him later and carried us south until sunset. I had the first shift of darkness, which was the easiest. Afterwards, I had a few beers before going to bed.

The women of my past tried to creep into my thoughts. I didn't need them clouding my mind on this trip. I tried to suppress the memories. Only one refused to leave me alone. The pretty face wearing glasses surrounded by auburn hair remained. I regretted not meeting up with her before leaving the west coast of Florida. I made a deal with the image of her in my mind. I'd look her up, if and when we survived this ordeal.

I stuck my head up on the bridge in the morning. Dan was awake and alert and still on course. I asked for a few minutes, and went below to check the bilge. All was well. I made a quick fuel calculation. We'd have to use some of the reserve fuel we'd added eventually, but we were fine for now. We had run twenty-four hours south will no ill effects. We still had a long way to go.

And so it went for the rest of the week. Four hours on, eight hours off. We'd skirted Cuban territorial waters by a comfortable margin. We were well off the coast of Mexico. We continued south outside the reef of Belize, and on to Columbia. Cartagena was a port city on the northern coast.

For thousands of years before the Spaniards first arrived, this area was populated by various native tribes. Just prior to the first invasion, the Karibs were the predominant people of the area. After a few failed attempts to settle this natural port, Spanish commander Pedro de Heredia finally conquered it. The town was named after Cartagena, Spain, where most of his crew had resided. The Spaniards set out plundering the rich gold and silver reserves. The dramatically increasing fame and wealth of the prosperous young city turned it into an attractive target for pirates and corsairs. After a serious pillaging by French raiders, the city set about strengthening itself with walled compounds and castles. The attacks continued, and more walls and forts were built. Later the French returned to invade yet again. The attack enabled a large group of pirates and thieves to destroy the city.

More fortresses were built, including a seven mile long wall surrounding the city. Numerous attempts were made to breach the new defenses, but none ever penetrated. The port itself remained a favorite stopover for pirates and privateers. We fit right in.

Our instructions were to anchor in the inner harbor, raise the Columbian flag, and wait. We did so. We watched the boat traffic coming and going from the docks of the city. We appeared to be one of a dozen vessels engaged in the same sort of commerce. Armed men in military style uniforms supervised the loading on the docks. Hard dark men carried their wares out to the waiting boats. I used binoculars to observe the transfers. The protocol seemed to be two men standing guard, weapons ready, on the receiving vessel, while two men took delivery of the goods. There were only three of us.

I had Robin fashion a sling for his shotgun out of some small line. He'd help me load, with the weapon strung across his back. Dan would stand by with his shiny new assault rifle. I had a pistol in the waistband of my pants. There was no reason for the delivery team to assault us. We had nothing of value, other than our vessel. We watched a few more deliveries. Nothing seemed out of order. Once loaded, the receiving vessels quickly pulled up anchor and left the harbor. We couldn't do that. We needed fuel.

Our turn came late in the afternoon. We all tried not to look nervous as we took delivery of a ton of coke. Robin even whistled while he worked. As soon as the last of the packages was loaded aboard, the delivery boat shoved off. I yelled to the men on board, who hadn't spoken a word.

"Fuel? Diesel? Petrol?" I hollered.

One of the men pointed to a rickety dock to our south. He spoke in broken English.

"No stay tonight," he said. "Thieves in night. Raiders come for you."

I nodded that I understood. My crew knew what to do. We pulled up anchor and made our way to the run-down fuel dock. I showed the attendant American hundred dollars bills and he hurried to fill our tanks. Dan and Robin stayed alert, weapons at the ready. We saw more hard dark men along the waterfront. They were watching us and talking amongst themselves. They knew what our cargo consisted of. I urged our man on the dock to hurry, but the fuel would only dispense so fast. The men on land began to gather together. I didn't see any weapons on them. The onboard tanks were full and we switched to filling the reserve. The dark men crept closer.

"Potential bogies approaching slowly from the west," I said to Dan and Robin. "Stay alert."

"Now we know why those other boats took off out of here so fast," said Dan.

"I didn't have enough information to make other arrangements," I answered. "Go to the bow and point right at them. Ward them off."

Robin stayed on the bridge with the shotgun. Dan went forward. I finished up fueling and paid the dockhand, before firing the engine. Dan pointed at the crowd of men. They jeered and shouted curses in a language I didn't understand. When Dan lowered his weapon to untie the bow line, they moved in his direction. Robin fired off a shot from the bridge. It was a warning. It hit no one. The men stopped. Dan threw off his line and pointed his weapon back at the men. I threw off the stern line and climbed quickly to the bridge.

The shotgun blast drew the attention of the uniformed men across the harbor. They were running our way. Once we cleared the dock, the threatening men scattered. The fuel attendant was alone on the dock when the soldiers arrived. We were two hundred yards away. They just stood and watched us leave. I wasted no time. I wound her up to seven knots immediately and left a bit of wake behind me to rock the remaining boats in the harbor.

We cleared the breakwater and headed for the open waters of the Caribbean Sea. No one said a word until the high fortresses of Cartagena disappeared behind us. I shut down the engine and left her drift.

"What's up?" said Robin.

"She probably needs some oil," I answered. "And we need to get all this shit stowed below. Better to do it without the engine running. Check the coolant too."

We worked quickly packing the hold with all that coke. Once each hatch was closed down, we covered it with old ropes, oil jugs, and assorted nautical items. After such a long trip, I would have liked to pay more attention to maintenance items, but now was not the time. She'd have to make it home the way she was. Nothing mechanically had gone wrong, but we still had a long way to go to deliver our payload.

Our four hour shifts resumed. The tension that hung in the air back in Cartagena never really left. We'd escaped with our lives and our cargo, but we were still nervous. Now we carried millions of dollars of illegal drugs in the hold. We had a thousand miles of open water to cross. We had to get into Biscayne Bay and make our meeting with Terry to offload the cocaine. I was worried about *Leap of Faith*. I was worried about bad weather. I was worried that the DEA would be waiting for us at the dock.

We chugged along day and night at seven knots, slowly clawing our way north. We rarely saw another vessel until we neared the reefs south of the Florida Keys. Spotting assorted shrimpers and fishing boats relieved a bit of the tension. We were nearing our destination. We couldn't stop anywhere along the way though. Our orders were to run straight for Biscayne Bay and make the transfer happen as soon as possible. Then we'd vacate the area, meeting back up in Tavernier later.

We almost made it to the dock without a hitch. With less than a mile to go, the engine sputtered and quit. We were adrift in the channel. We could see our destination, but we were slowly drifting away from it. I thought for a minute. I hadn't had a lick of trouble out of this motor since it was installed. Then it occurred to me. We'd traveled over two thousand miles on a single fuel filter. It was probably just clogged. I had spares. I took a quick look around and developed a new worry. We'd soon drift into shallow water and become grounded. We couldn't let that happen, not with a ton of blow down below.

I dropped anchor right there in the channel. I was an expert fuel filter changer. I'd done it many times. I grabbed what I needed and hurried below. The filter was switched out and the fuel lines were bled. I bled the air out of the injector pump and yelled for Robin to start the engine. It fired right up. I yelled for Dan to pull the anchor. When I climbed out of the bilge we were back underway towards the dock. As we approached, I saw Terry standing there. No one else was in sight. We nudged the pilings and tied off.

"What the hell was that?" asked Terry. "You scared the shit out of me when you stopped out there."

"Engine quit," I answered. "Fuel filter. Long trip. Where's the unloading crew?"

"We're it," he said. "I'll back the van down and we'll get you off-loaded."

"Is the coast clear?" I asked. "We're all pretty nervous about this part."

"We've got Monroe County's finest watching the road," he answered. "Relax."

I'd almost forgotten how far Bald Mark's influence traveled. The risk had been out at sea. We were safe now, assuming all went as planned. No waterborne law enforcement agency had seen any threat from my old trawler. We'd walked a boat load of cocaine into Miami, right under their nose. It almost felt good.

We transferred to drugs to the van without incident. Terry drove off like he was carrying groceries. The three of us looked at each other and shrugged.

"Let's take this old girl back to Tavernier," I said. "Drinks are on me."

The weight of our fear and tension fell away. We'd done it. I can't say I was proud of what we'd done, but I was proud of my friends. I was proud of my boat. Back at the marina we invaded the Tiki Bar. Our spirits lifted as we drank. Dan made a toast to a mission accomplished. Robin made a toast to good friends. I made a toast to *Leap of Faith*. We switched from beer to rum and got fall-down sloppy drunk.

Terry arrived and we all staggered to my boat. The cash was divvied up. We all got quiet and stared at the piles of money. Our lives would be changed forever. Three poor boat bums could now do whatever they chose. It was time to go home.

Going Home

We all met up in Boot Key Harbor before heading north. I wanted one last visit to Dockside before we left. I didn't know if, or when, I'd ever be back. I was disappointed. I recognized none of the servers. Eric Stone was on the road playing his music somewhere. The new waitresses were not attractive in any way. Nice enough gals, but not much to look at. I ordered a Yuengling draft, but was told they were out. I had to settle for a Bud Light.

Diver Dan and Robin arrived. We took a table in the corner and discussed our travel plans. After two weeks at sea, no one was interested in a long non-stop run to Fort Myers Beach. We decided to break it up into three legs. We'd run eight hours until we reached a place to anchor off the coast of the mainland. Then we'd travel ten hours up to Marco Island. From there it was only another six hours into Matanzas Pass. I'd done it a dozen times.

The next morning, three boats said farewell to the Keys and started their journey across Florida Bay towards the Everglades. Once we cleared the shoals north of the Seven Mile Bridge, Robin raised his sails and veered west to catch the wind. Dan and I plodded along at seven knots, running a straight line for our destination. The day was bright and clear. Winds were moderate out of the east. A light chop disturbed the surface of the clear water.

It was good to be alone with *Miss Leap*. I listened to the noises she made. I tuned into the steady purr of her diesel engine. I patted the dashboard and spoke to her.
"Good job, Leap," I said. "I promise we'll take it easy after this."

She hummed along happily. Her bow shoved the waves aside as we plowed towards home. Later in the afternoon we approached the coast near Little Shark River. The tall mangroves blocked us from the east winds, so I dropped anchor just offshore. Dan was right behind me. Robin showed up about an hour later. We all stayed aboard our own boats for the night. Maybe they were glad to be alone again too.

The next day went smoothly, until we ran into a storm just off Marco Island. It was a typical afternoon thunder boomer. We all bounced about and got wet for thirty minutes and then it was gone. Three anchors were dropped in Factory Bay. Three solo sailors sat on their boats alone for another evening.

The following day we all arrived together at Fort Myers Beach. Dan and Robin slowly made their way past the mooring field and into the back water where they'd left One-legged Beth. I chose to pick up a ball. I wanted a hot shower and a cold beer. When I made my way up the steps to the Upper Deck, Jennifer was there with a smile and a quick hug.

"Where have you been?" she asked. "You've been gone forever. Have you had another adventure?"

I think I visibly winced when she said "another adventure". I'd been able to avoid the memory of Joy's death for almost a year. I shook it off and returned her smile.

"Just keeping a low profile," I said. "Trying to stay out of the public eye."

"I'm glad you decided to pay us a visit," she said. "Hanging around this time?"

She gave me an expectant look, like maybe we could hook up after all this time. I wasn't averse to the idea, but I'd made up my mind to give it a try with Taylor.

"I think I'm going up to Punta Gorda soon," I said. "There's some friends I'd like to see."

"Enjoy your stay," she offered. "You know where to find me."

"It's good to see you again, Jennifer," I said.

"Always good to see you, Breeze," she replied.

I drank my beer and thought about the future. I had more than four hundred thousand dollars in cash stashed about the boat. In a few weeks, my probation officer would sign off on my ultimate release from the Florida judicial system. I was a free man. I was also a wealthy man once again. I just needed to figure out how to hold onto my wealth this time. I left a twenty dollar tip for a three dollar beer and waved goodbye to Jennifer.

"Keep smiling, girl," I said.

"Come back and see us," she replied.

Diver Dan and Robin found One-legged Beth in a state of disarray. The outboard on her skiff had caught fire and she had been stuck on the boat for a week. She hadn't showered. She was out of food. She'd been living on water and dope for three days straight. She was weak and disoriented. The woman needed adult supervision. When I heard about her condition, I went to the grocery store and loaded up on good food. I didn't know what she liked, but I figured she could use a good steak and some potatoes. I knew that Dan and Robin would take care of her, but I slipped a few hundred dollar bills in with her groceries anyway.

We all sat with her that night and told our tales. We left nothing out. We embellished a little. Dan had a way to tell a story with dry humor. Robin was more excitable, especially when he told about shooting those pirates off the Marquesas. I tried to stick to the facts, but couldn't help making the long trips back and forth to Columbia seem even more arduous than they really were.

Finally, I told them all I was moving on. Beth was disappointed. Dan had figured I wouldn't stay all along. Robin understood. I got man-hugs from Dan and Robin. I got a long girl-hug from Beth and a kiss on the cheek.

"Don't you be a stranger, Breeze," she said. "You've always got friends here."

"You be good now," I answered. "Stay out of trouble."

I left the unlikely trio to catch up on things. I wished them all well and quietly made my way back to the boat. I sat alone on the aft deck and watched the cars going over the Matanzas Bridge. I had a slight regret about leaving my friends behind. I had a slight regret about not taking up with Jennifer, while I had the chance. Neither regret was enough to hold me here. I was moving on. I'd completed this episode of my life. New episodes were on the horizon.

I could have made Punta Gorda in seven hours, but I stopped over in Pelican Bay. I wanted to clear my head, and decompress a little. I didn't have a plan. I could have stayed for a day, or a week. The first night I decided to bring the last of Laura's ashes out for a little communion. Her memory was no longer ever-present, but I could summon her when I felt the need. I just sat there watching the pelicans dive for a while. I drank beer and waited for sunset. Eventually, I began to sense her presence. I didn't feel admonished for neglecting her lately. I didn't sink into guilt over my recent coke smuggling career, though I knew she would disapprove. We were no longer one. Physically, she was gone. In my mind, I still had a link to her energy. I tried to absorb it. I closed my eyes and let myself float.

She didn't speak to me. I didn't see her ghost, but she was there. It wasn't magic, or telepathy. I could just feel her.
"I think I'm past the worst of it," I said aloud. "I can go legit now. I'm okay on money. I don't feel the urge to seek adventure. I don't want to stay hidden from the world anymore either. I'm ready for a new life. I just don't know what to do next."
I stayed silent after that. I didn't get specific instructions. I got a good feeling though. Laura was telling me that it would all be okay. Things would work out. She wanted me to move on with my life. Seek out some meaning. Do something good. She had faith in me.

"Thank you, Laura. I'll always love you."

Empty beer cans rolling around on deck woke me in the morning. There must have been a dozen of them. A stunning sunrise broke above Punta Blanca Island. The first rays of light beamed onto *Leap of Faith* like a spotlight on a Broadway stage. A tarpon surged out of the water in an impossibly athletic leap. Sea gulls made their sea gull sounds.

I had survived to live this moment in spite of all my poor decisions. Life was good, for a change. I finally felt like I could move forward. I didn't have to hide any longer. I wasn't running from anything. All the illegal substances that had been carried aboard my vessel had been replaced with cold, hard cash. I didn't need to convalesce here at all. I was ready.

I didn't even eat breakfast. I pulled up anchor and made my way into Charlotte Harbor, bound for Punta Gorda. Three hours later, I passed under the bridges of Route 41 and into the Peace River. The first thing I noticed was Cross-Eyed John's boat on a mooring ball. I called Laishley Park Marina on the VHF and got my slip assignment. My new home was in slip D-3.

Cross-Eyed John

I'd first met John some years back in Gilchrest Park. He had his boat anchored just offshore. I had taken my dinghy to the beach to scrape the barnacles off the bottom. It was in bad shape. John approached me with a proposal. There was a homeless dude in the park that would do the job for me, for a little cash. He took me to meet the guy and we came to an agreement. John helped him scrape the barnacles, but wouldn't take any money.

We talked for a bit and I heard some of John's story. He had been homeless in the Keys for five years. He'd had a tough time with some tough people. He drank too much. He smoked a lot of dope. He occasionally got himself arrested for disorderly conduct or battery. Someone taught him to weave hats and flowers out of palm fronds. He used his new skill to earn a living selling his wares on Duval Street. He was good at it. He suddenly had a good income. He spent every penny on booze and dope, not just for himself, but for his ever-growing troupe of homeless friends.

One day he decided he needed a change. He saved up enough money to buy a small sailboat. His plan was to escape his homelessness, and his addictions, by sailing far away from the Keys. John had never sailed before, but he was undaunted. The hailing port of his new boat was painted on the transom. It said Punta Gorda. John chose Punta Gorda as his new home. He ran aground often. He got lost. Fogged socked him in somewhere off the coast of Marco. Somehow, he made it. He dropped his anchor off Gilchrest Park. He'd been sober for weeks. He was going to AA meetings. A temp agency was giving him some work.

It didn't last. When I went to the park to sell my homemade rum, John was first in line. He'd fallen off the wagon. Hell, he burned the damned wagon. He had a new gang of homeless buddies. I used him to negotiate with them on the sale of my rum. A bar fight got him arrested. The bums wore on him. He tried to quit drinking again, because he recognized the trouble he was about to face. He'd been there before. When he went back on the wagon, I lost the bums as customers. They preferred to rough me up and take the rum for nothing.

John was just one of those people who should never touch a drop of alcohol. When he was sober, he really was a decent guy. He had a good heart. He knew right from wrong. When he was drunk, he was quick to fight. He made some astonishing bad decisions. He went to jail. I had an understanding with him. We could relate with each other about one thing. The only thing separating him from homelessness was his boat. No matter how bad it got, he always had a home. He loved his little boat as much as I loved mine.

Eventually, he caused enough trouble in town, and the marine cop asked him to relocate. He stopped into Pelican Bay to tell me he was moving up to Sarasota. I lost touch with him after that. I hadn't seen him in two years. He must have seen me entering the marina, because he hopped in his dinghy and came right into my slip to say hi. He'd cut his long hair and looked presentable, but he confessed he was drinking again. He said he had no friends. He'd pissed off half of them and beaten up the rest.

He'd sobered up for a while in Sarasota. He got a job at a restaurant and had high hopes. He'd even gotten a girlfriend. The next thing he knew, he was drinking again. She drank a lot too. She hadn't believed his stories about how bad he'd been as a drunk. She pulled him right back into it. His employer got around to running a background check and decided they had to let him go. He hadn't listed all his arrests on his application, they said. The relationship got crazy. The girl turned out to be a nut job. Cross-Eyed John wasn't exactly mentally stable himself. She charged him with kidnapping and battery. He was arrested yet again.

That case was still outstanding when John found trouble again. He came into the marina one day towing a Boston Whaler skiff behind his dinghy. It was beaten and battered, but he was proud of it.

"I got it for nothing," he told me. "I was doing some odd jobs, cleaning up foreclosed properties. The realtor sent a letter to the debtor telling him to get this boat off the property. He never showed up, so they told me to take it if I wanted. I just need a motor for it."

It just so happened, that I had recently purchased a new motor for my dinghy. The old Mercury had given me one too many heartbreaks lately. It would pair up perfectly with John's rundown skiff.

"I tell you what John," I started. "That old Merc is worth close to a thousand bucks. I could sell it in one day on Craigslist. I'll sell it to you for six hundred, if you've got the cash."

"I'll give you five hundred for it," he said.

"Deal," I answered. "Come back in the morning and we'll install it."

"You the man, Breeze," he said.

He left the skiff tied to the dinghy dock and drove off, shin deep in empty beer cans.

The next morning, I put the motor on his skiff by myself. As I sat down on the dock to get in his boat, I found a wallet laying there. It was Johns. A quick peak revealed over a thousand bucks inside. I put it in my pocket and tried to start the motor. It didn't start. I pulled, and pulled, and pulled. It refuse to fire. This was the reason I wanted to part ways with it. I got my tools and took the motor back off the skiff. I cleaned the carburetor. I pulled and cleaned the plugs. I cleaned the fuel filter. It would not run.

Cross-Eyed John showed up, beer in hand, telling a sob story.

"Man, I can't pay you," he started. "I lost my wallet."

I pulled his wallet out of my pocket and handed it to him.

"My money is still in it," he said. "I can't believe it."

"What? You think I'd steal the money you're supposed to pay me?" I asked.

"Nah, man, I know you wouldn't take my money," he replied. "But somebody else might have."

He tried pulling the starter rope a dozen times. No go. I tried again. Nothing doing.

"I ain't paying if it don't run," he said.

"Of course not," I said. "I'll get it going. Just let me take a break. Come back later. I'll fool with it some more."

I was really frustrated. I could take John in small doses, but I didn't need him hanging around watching my every move. He was drinking heavily early in the morning. I got him to leave and thought over my problem. It dawned on me what was wrong. I spent the rest of the afternoon working on that stubborn outboard. It finally sputtered to life. With a little fine tuning, it eventually ran smoothly. I hoped to God that this would be my last battle with that cantankerous beast.

I drove John's new skiff with his new motor out to his sail boat. He was sleeping off his buzz, naked. After he put some shorts on, he saw what was going on.
"Holy shit, you got it running," he said. "Take me for a ride."
I drove him around the harbor. The Mercury pushed the little skiff along just fine.
"Take me to your boat," he said. "I'll drive it on back out."

He was happy with the motor, and with me, for getting it running so well. He paid me the cash and drove away happy. A little while later he came back and presented me with a six-pack of beer.
"This motor is awesome, Breeze," he said. "I'm tickled with it. You are the king. Thanks so much for hooking me up so good."

"No problem," I replied. "I hope it works out for you."

He was smiling like a kid at a birthday party. He had a new toy and he went off to play with it. I didn't see him again until the next day. He showed up with a story to tell.

"Man, I was having so much fun," he said. "I had a cooler full of beer. I was running all over the harbor just having a blast. Then I ran out of gas. I drank till I passed out. I woke up this morning all the way up the Myakka River at El Jobean."

"I told you it wasn't full of gas," I said.

"Yea, well, I forgot all about it," he said. "I was having too much fun."

"How'd you get back?" I asked.

Some fella over there towed my skiff and took me to Fisherman's Village. I got some gas and made it back here just now. I gotta get some more beer."

"You're going to get busted with that expired registration," I warned him. "That and all those empty cans will get you in trouble."

"Don't sweat it, Breeze," he said. "I'm on a roll. With this skiff things are going to be different. I can get a job. Things are turning my way for once."

I didn't want to bust his happy bubble, so I let it drop. He went off to get more beer and I forgot about it. A few hours later, he was in handcuffs.

He had come zooming along in a no-wake zone on his way to the marina. An FWC officer pulled him over. The first thing she noticed was the expired registration. It hadn't been legal since 2008. She took him into the free dock at the boat ramp. The second thing she noticed was the collection of empty Budweiser cans on the floor of the skiff. She thought he might be intoxicated, so she gave him a breathalyzer. She was right. He failed the test. She called the Sheriff's office and half a dozen cops arrived. Cars, trucks and boats pulled up to the ramp. The only thing missing was a horse. Someone called in the FL numbers on the skiff. It had been reported stolen the day before. Cross-Eyed John was in deep shit.

By some strange coincidence, the previous owner of the skiff was having lunch at Harpoon Harry's, which is part of Fisherman's Village. He'd seen the skiff when John came in to get fuel. He'd written it off, but now that it was right in front of him, he decided he wanted it back. John tried to explain how he'd come into possession of the skiff, but the cops weren't buying it. Off he went to jail. I watched as the Sheriff's deputy pulled the skiff to the ramp and unloaded all of John's junk into a truck. They took the Mercury. I'd been drinking myself by this time, so I stayed out of it.

Amongst John's belongings, the cops discovered a large amount of marijuana. It looked to be about two pounds worth.

Cross-Eyed John was in deeper shit. I watched from the dock as the dude from Harpoon Harry's came to reclaim the little boat. I felt really bad for John, but he'd done it to himself. All of his hopes for the future were down the drain.

Three days went by before I saw John again. He paid his own bond. The realtor had come to vouch for his version of how he got the skiff. The theft charge was dropped. He was still on the hook for boating under the influence, and possession of marijuana with intent to distribute. He'd be going away for a while, once it went to court. He had no way to get back out to his boat, so I gave him a ride. He was really down. He'd screwed up big this time.

I was worried about him, but there was only so much I could do. I went back to my beer drinking and tried to think happy thoughts. That night, John tried to kill himself. The plan should have worked. He positioned a portable generator so that the exhaust would fill the cabin of his sail boat. He sat below and drank himself to sleep. Just as he dozed off, he heard the carbon monoxide detector beeping its alarm. He thought he'd never wake up.

Maybe God was looking down on him, I don't know. They say he takes care of fools and drunks. John was both. Soon after he drifted off into what he thought would be his last sleep, the generator ran out of gas. He'd forgotten to put fuel in it, just as he'd done with the skiff. He was surprised to be alive in the morning. He didn't know if he should kick himself for botching the job, or celebrate his failure to commit suicide. He came to me to talk.

"Jesus, John," I scolded. "You can't do that. I know all of this sucks, but some day you'll have to answer to God."

"I know it's a mortal sin," he told me. "I guess it wasn't meant to be."

"I'm glad you're still alive," I said. "Maybe God was trying to tell you something."

"I don't know if I can keep going," he started. "I won't do well in prison. I can't lose my boat. I just don't think I could take it."

"Have you thought about raising your sails and running away?" I asked.

"I don't have much money left, Breeze," he answered. "They got me good with the dope. They'd catch me soon enough. I've always faced my problems."

I had not always faced my problems. I had ran and hidden and kept my head in the sand. The problems found me anyway. I was only able to face them, because I had money. Without the money, I'd be in jail instead of giving bad advice to a cross-eyed drunk.

He stayed for a couple hours, drinking beer and telling me his life story. Kids had picked on him due to his eyes. He took boxing lessons, and learned to fight back when they teased him. He learned some tricks on the streets as a young man. In the Keys he'd had to fight to stay alive. He'd seen people killed, over their Social Security checks. Once he pulled up to a dinghy dock, to find a man beating someone with an oar. He managed to take the weapon from him, getting whacked in the head in the process. When he saw his own blood, he'd beaten the man senseless. He'd been charged with battery in that incident. The original victim had disappeared.

He told a string of sad sack stories. Sometimes he was in the wrong place at the wrong time. More often, he was just drunk and mean. His life on the street had hardened him. He said he could cope better on the boat. He wasn't so mad all the time. He was taking medication that seemed to work. He'd come so close to digging his way out. Now the hole was caving in on him.

"Look, Breeze," he said. "I'm going away for a long time. You're my friend. Hell, you're my only friend. I want to give you my stuff."

"What stuff?" I asked.

"I'm giving you the Mercury back," he began. "I'm not asking you to buy it back. I'm giving it to you. I also have the little Nissan outboard, a generator, and some electronics."

"I can't take all your stuff, John," I said. "It doesn't feel right."

"None of this feels right," he replied. "But I'd rather give it to you than lose it all."

"You think it over," I told him. "Give it a few days. See how the charges work out."

"They want to know where the dope came from," he said. "I can't tell them. I can't rat. I'd probably get killed if I ratted."

"I know where you're coming from," I said. "Just try to take it easy. Don't think about killing yourself. Don't even think about it."

"Thanks, Breeze," he said. "I feel better just talking to you. Maybe I'll be okay. The only person that ever listened to me before was that crazy bitch up in Sarasota."

"Keep the faith, brother," I said.

We shook hands and he slowly motored out of the marina. I hoped he'd be alive the next day.

Taylor

"This can't be Breeze," Taylor answered when I called. "The Breeze I knew would have called at least once over the past freaking year."

"Yea, about that," I stuttered. "I could tell you all about it over dinner."

"One day you're all over the news," she continued. "The next you're a ghost. Disappeared, vanished, not even a goodbye Taylor."

"I know it's a poor excuse," I replied. "But I couldn't handle all the attention. Seeing myself on TV freaked me out, so I laid low for a while."

"A whole damn year?" she asked. "Why should I even talk to you? I saved your bacon. I thought we might have a little something brewing between us. Then you just bail on me."

This was not the reception I had expected. Something else was wrong. I didn't know her all that well, but I could hear it in her voice. She was wound tight and troubled. She was also taking it out on me. I must have picked a bad time to call.

"Is something wrong?" I asked. "I mean other than me being an asshole."

"Oh Breeze," she started. "It's been awful. I can't tell you on the phone. I don't know if I can tell you at all."

"Dinner?" I asked.

"Where are you?" she asked in reply.

"At the marina," I said. "I'm here to see you. I plan to stay."

"Okay, I'll come there," she said. "You just want to go up to the Crabhouse?"

"The only thing they do well is sushi," I answered.

"I could go for that. I'll see you at six," she said.

I had just enough time to get cleaned up and put on my best shirt. I always felt weird when I was freshly showered and shaved. I spent so much time unshaven and dirty it was more natural than being clean. I looked at myself in the mirror with a critical eye. Some wrinkles around my eyes had gotten deeper. I was darker than most would consider healthy. I kept my hair short these days. It was just easier to deal with, and cooler that way. I'd changed a lot over the past five years. I'd gotten leaner. It gave me an edgy look. My eyes were still a brilliant blue though. They were my best feature. Chicks always dug my eyes. I decided I'd get an inside table and not wear my sunglasses.

I experienced butterflies like a teenage boy when I saw her coming down the dock. Her auburn hair and those glasses were unmistakable. Long legs terminated under a short skirt on one end, and into high heels on the other. She carried her thin frame in a proud posture. She was not overtly sexual, unless you were into librarian types. Other than the short skirt, she was very conservative. Her business jacket was buttoned up high, showing no cleavage. When she reached my slip, I stepped off the boat to help her aboard.

"Still the prettiest lawyer lady I know," I said.

"You clean up pretty good yourself, for a boat bum," she answered.

We didn't hug or kiss or even shake hands. We just stood there for a few seconds. I put my hands on her shoulders and tried to look into her eyes. She put her head down and stared at her shoes.

"Are you all right?" I asked.

"I want to be," she answered. "But I'm not. I can't shake it."

"Can't shake what?" I asked. "What happened?"

"I keep trying to erase it from my mind," she began. "I don't want to relive it. Breeze, I was um, assaulted. You know, sexually."

I didn't know what to say. I felt I had to say something, but the right words wouldn't come. I pulled her to me and hugged her gently. She began to cry softly, her head resting on my shoulder. She continued to sob and I continued to hold her. She didn't wail. She didn't cry out loud. I could barely hear her sniffles. I could feel little tremors. I felt helpless and clumsy, standing there on the dock with a professional woman putting a puddle of tears into my pocket.

"Would you like a drink?" I offered.

"Yes," she answered. "That would be great. Sorry to be a sissy."

"Beer, wine or rum?" I asked.

"I'd love a few ounces of rum over ice," she answered. "Calms the nerves."

I fixed her drink and got myself a beer. I felt it best to stay sober for this. Her tears made her no less lovely. I was a really good listener, but I still had no idea what to say. When I returned, she changed the subject entirely.

"So where have you been hiding all this time?" she asked.

"I was down in the Keys," I answered. "I stayed holed up in a secluded marina the whole time."

"And you could afford this?" she asked suspiciously.

"Actually, the slip was free," I replied. "I did some odd jobs for the owner."

She knew I wasn't telling her the whole truth. I knew that she knew. She gave me a crooked look, but let it drop. She was extremely quick minded, and she knew enough about me to assume a few things. She hadn't blinked an eye when we first met due to my arrest. Two pounds of dope hadn't bothered her any. She remained professional while being sly at the same time. She didn't even act too surprised when I was able to produce the bribes necessary for an easy sentence.

There was more to her than met the eye. As a defense attorney, she lived in a shadowy world of criminals of all types. She put off a virtuous air, but I knew better. The immediate problem though, was the assault. How bad had it been? How would she handle it going forward? I didn't know any of the specifics, and I wasn't going to ask. She could tell me if she wanted, or not. Meanwhile, my chances of romance in the near future had diminished greatly. I wasn't about to make any moves on a recent rape victim. I had some problems with virtue myself, but that was a line I wouldn't cross.

She sipped her chilled rum and looked around at the other boats in the marina. I held my gaze on her for a minute, studying her. Her skin was very white, like most women with reddish hair. She had just a hint of freckles here and there. I suspected a little sunshine would accentuate them. She had a habit of tucking her hair behind her ears when it got in her face. She reminded me a bit of Jennifer Garner. Her jaw clenched and unclenched under her smooth skin. She was chewing on a problem.

"Look Taylor," I began. "I wasn't lying when I said I came here to see you. Now that I'm here, if there is anything I can do to help, please let me know. I don't know what else to say right now, other than I will be here for you, if you need me."

"What I really want to do is run away from it all," she said. "I just want to hide from the world for a little while. You, my friend, are an expert at that."

"Why yes," I said. "I have some expertise in that area. Part of me thinks we'd be a little uncomfortable alone together on this boat, but part of me thinks it would be absolutely wonderful."

"I'm not talking about a naked romp, Breeze. You aren't Travis McGee. I'm not one of his little bunnies that needs fixing."

"Of course," I said, in self-defense. "You're a tough cookie. Maybe I can get you to fix me while we're gone."

"So you'll take me away?" she asked. "I've got two weeks of vacation time. I just need to tidy up a few things at the office first."

"On one condition," I said. "You have to promise to wear nothing but bikinis, or less."

She laughed, but soon turned serious. She was still working her jaw nervously.

"You'll have to be patient with me, Breeze," she said. "I'm not ready. I'll work it out. Give me time."

"I once carried a hot little Cuban gal halfway around the world, and never touched her," I bragged. "She was nowhere near as hot as you, but I'll do my best to remain a gentleman."

She blushed a little bit at my blatant flattery. She even smiled a little.

"There's so much I don't know about you," she said. "I never know what to expect out of you next."

"We have two weeks to get acquainted," I said. "No pressure. My vessel is your vessel."

"Thanks, Breeze," she said. "I feel better just talking to you."

"You're the second person to tell me that this week," I told her.

It looked like I had found my calling. I could just sit and listen to people. I didn't actually fix anything or provide any physical help. I just listened, throwing in a word or two now and then. I didn't judge, or offer advice, or pretend that I knew what to do about it. I could just be there. That was good. The only other thing I was good at was running and hiding. Those skills would help with Taylor's situation in the short term. I figured I'd have to hone my listening skills for the long term.

She showed up wearing shorts and a little white tank top. It was the first time I'd ever seen her without business attire. She had small but perky breasts, with nipples that poked at the thin fabric. I took her bag and showed her around.

"You'll sleep here in the portside berth," I said. "I'll sleep up there on the settee. I wake up very early and drink coffee. I'll try to be quiet. After my coffee I'll be taking a poop here in the head, right across from where you'll be sleeping. Consider that a warning. We'll share cooking and cleaning duties, but you're free to do whatever you want otherwise. There is no schedule. This ain't no cruise ship with planned activities to keep the sheep occupied."

"Aye aye, captain," she said with a quick salute.

"One more thing," I said. "You will hereby change into a bikini, as per our agreement."

"I promised no such thing," she giggled.

"This vessel will remain in the slip until all females aboard are properly attired," I insisted.

She went off to change while I warmed up the engine and prepared to toss the lines. She came out of the berth in a sweet little bikini and slowly turned in a circle for my inspection. I liked what I saw. She had a narrow waist and a flat belly. There was no evidence that she'd ever given birth to a child. There was the slightest curve at the hips, with thin thighs and shapely legs. If nothing happened between us over the next two weeks, at least I'd get to look at her.

Cross-Eyed John pulled up in his dinghy. When he saw Taylor in her bikini, I swear his eyes straightened out for second. I introduced them, and told him we were about to leave.

"I won't stay long," he said. "I just wanted to give you an update. I haven't had a drink in four days and my head is pretty clear. I've got a plan to save my boat, and I think I can save the other stuff too. I've got a hearing next week, so we'll see what exactly I get charged with. I think I'm going to be okay, Breeze."

"Good news, man," I said. "You look good. You sound better."

"Thanks again, for, you know, being my friend."

"Keep your head on straight," I said. "You can get through this."

"All right, brother," he said. "I'll let you loose. Have a nice trip."

"I'll be back in two weeks," I said. "Catch you later. Stay out of trouble."

Taylor showed no signs of the distress as we departed. She seemed so much younger in her less serious mode. She dropped the strict posture and skipped about like a school girl.

"Are you helping that guy out somehow?" she asked.

"I didn't set out to help him, to be honest," I answered. "He sort of attached himself to me. I listened to his troubles. Hell, I listened to his life story. He just needed someone to talk to."

"This is the essence of Breeze," she said.

I said, "Huh?"

"You are a conundrum, a riddle," she began. "You obviously have a good heart. You're a kind and decent man, but you find trouble, or it finds you."

"I could say the same thing about Cross-Eyed John," I said.

"Maybe that's why you're willing to help him," she answered.

"I hadn't really thought of that," I said. "He just came to me and I listened. I didn't really do anything."

"You didn't judge, because you don't want to be judged," she said. "You've done some things too."

"That's all behind me now," I said. "Believe me. From here on out I'm Mr. Law Abiding Citizen."

"You know how many times I've heard something similar from clients?" she laughed. "I have to admit something though. I find it sexy. Bad boy attraction and all that."

Rather than say something stupid, I busied myself with gauges and knobs. It was a quick three hour run to Pelican Bay, where she could hide from the world to her heart's delight. No mention was made of her deeper troubles. We continued to ignore the elephant in the room for the first week.

She fixed breakfast and I did the dishes. I cooked dinner and she cleaned up afterwards. We swam and walked on the beach. Mostly I sat in a chair and read a book while she walked alone. Her fair skin could only take an hour or so of exposure to the harsh Florida sun. She'd spent too much time in offices and courtrooms. I got to observe her bikini body in the morning for a bit, but she was forced to cover up before she burned. As predicted, when she developed a bit of a tan, her freckles popped out. She hated them. I thought they were cute.

I took her to see the manatees. We chased dolphins in the dinghy. We joined the weekend party on the sand bar. We had a cheeseburger at Cabbage Key. We sat in deck chairs, drinks in hand, to watch the sun set over the Gulf.

"This," she said. "This is how life should be lived. I love this."

We'd shared zero intimacy so far. She had made no indication that she wanted to talk, or that she wanted anything out of me. I took a chance anyway.

"This is the life I've lead for the past five years," I said. "This bay, this spot right here, is my happy place. The only thing that keeps me away, is the fact that I'm alone. It's so much better when it's shared with someone."

"I don't know anything about your life, Breeze," she said. "Why you're alone, what happened to you, how you got here, it's all a mystery."

"And I know nothing of yours," I countered. "We're a mystery to each other."

"Part of me wants to keep it that way," she said. "Part of me wants to tell you everything."

"I'm a great listener," I teased.

"You first," she demanded. "I'm not sure I'm ready to spill my guts."

I thought it over for a minute. She waited in silence. Maybe if I told her my story, she'd tell me hers. If I talked freely, she would do the same. The last thing I wanted to hear, were the details of a vicious rape, but if getting it off her chest would help, I could listen.

It took several hours, and plenty of beer. I started with Laura's death. I admitted to embezzling from my employer. I told her how I ran away, bought the boat, and disappeared from society. I told her about growing dope and cooking rum. I told her about the bums in the park, and how I'd met Cross-Eyed John. I told her about Andi, and spreading ashes in the Caribbean Sea. I told her about Yolanda, Bald Mark, and Enrique. I told her about watching Joy die on a street in Miami. I almost told her all of it. I stopped short of the cocaine smuggling. She sensed I was leaving something out. She really was quite perceptive. She was also as good a listener as I was. I appreciated that.

"My life hasn't been nearly as exciting as yours," she began. "It's been pretty privileged as a matter of fact. I haven't suffered any great loss. My parents are still alive and wealthy. I excelled in school and went to a great college. Mom and Dad paid for law school. It's all been quite charmed really. I can't figure out where it went wrong."

"Sounds pretty good to me," I said. "Why do you say it went wrong?"

"Because I'm alone too, Breeze," she answered. "You don't have a monopoly on loneliness. I was focused. I worked hard. I strove for excellence. I never made time for relationships. I never met anyone with the same drive, the same level of intellect, or the same goals in life. I dismissed anyone who tried to get inside my bubble. I thought I'd come to terms with it, until, well, until it happened."

"The assault?" I asked.

"We can stop playing games now," she said. "I was raped okay?"

"You don't have to talk about it if you don't want to," I offered.

"Here's the deal," she started. "I was kicking life's ass. I was a damn good lawyer, making a ton of money. I have a nice home, hotshot sports car and anything I want. I didn't need a man to fulfill me. I could do anything, by myself. I was a strong and independent career woman with unlimited potential. Screw men."

"And then?"

"And then some animal destroyed my illusions," she said. "He made me helpless. He broke me down and controlled me for his own violent pleasure. I was reduced to a weak, whimpering, scared little girl. I was afraid. I'm still afraid. I lost my edge. I've lost my confidence. People whisper behind my back. She's the one that got raped. The worst part is, when I go home at night, I'm all alone. All that special shit I have, the great life I've built for myself, I have no one to share it with. Kind of like you and this place, this life."

"I could make a case that we're meant for each other," I said.

"We're from different worlds, Breeze," she said. "I envy your world, but it doesn't mix well with mine."

"I can't fault your logic," I said. "But sometimes you have to forget logic. Have you ever listened to your gut, or your heart, instead of your head?"

"No, never," she replied frankly. "It's not part of the plan. I can't get sidetracked by some impossible dream. I can just dip my toes in it for two weeks, than go back to work."

"Then I will stay at the marina," I said. "Will you see me when you have time?"

"I don't know," she answered. "You frighten me. Not in a scary way, but because I could see myself just throwing caution to the wind and falling hard for you. You are so completely different from anyone I've ever met, but I sense danger. You're trouble, Mr. Breeze."

"Look, Taylor," I said. "I finally reached a place where I can settle down. I'd like to have real friends, make real commitments. I need to rejoin society and live a more normal life. I can do that in Punta Gorda. I'm serious about this."

"Then you wouldn't be a sexy, dangerous man anymore," she said. "Your difference is part of what makes you attractive. You're a wild card, living free. All those women you told me about, that's what they saw in you."

I almost agreed with her. That is how I saw myself. That's what I'd become. I was proud of it. I wore it like a badge. I'd been places and seen things that most folks never will experience. I'd lived outside the borders. I'd been a rebel in a society that crushes rebellion. She was right, except for one thing. I was no rebel when I married Laura. I worked a nine-to-five job and climbed the corporate ladder. I was a model citizen. I was a faithful and loving husband. Laura loved me for what I was then.

"There was Laura," was all I could say.

I wanted to cry. I don't know what came over me. One minute I was trying to get in a hot chick's pants, the next minute I missed my wife so bad it crushed my soul. My chest heaved as I did my best not to break down in front of Taylor. She reached over and took my hand in hers.

"Are you okay?" she asked softly.

"I'm sorry," I responded. "Every time I think I've overcome my grief, something triggers it again. I've gotten better. I've moved on, but I miss her."

"Some couple we'd make," she said. "Broken and more broken."

"Two lost souls swimming in a fishbowl, year after year," I sang, badly.

She gave me a little punch on the shoulder and pulled me up out of the chair.

"Come on," she said. "Let's go to bed."

"Let's?" I asked. "Like in us, together?"

"Us," she answered. "I want to experience dangerous Breeze, before he becomes boring, everyman Breeze."

I couldn't argue with that. It was just the medicine I needed.

There's this thing about redheads that I found to be consistently true, in my younger years. As a rule, they are totally uninhibited in bed. Buckled up, prim, Sunday school teachers, turned into animals once the clothes come off. If a girl has red hair, it's a good bet she'll rock your world when the lights go out. Taylor was no different, except she preferred the lights on. She took the lead, guiding me to fulfill her needs. I was happy to oblige. It took every ounce of my self-control to maintain. She worked me to the edge, teasing me. We moved well together, sensing each other's wants. It was free and easy. It was as natural as I'd ever known, like we were indeed meant for each other.

"So that's sex," she said afterwards.
"You're no virgin," I replied.
"No, I mean real sex. Breeze, you were awesome."
"We," I said. "We were awesome. It takes two to tango."
"Yes, yes, yes," she squealed. "We were awesome. I could get used to that."
"So does this mean you'll see me, back in Punta Gorda?" I asked.
"Yes," she answered. "You can be sexy dangerous Breeze in bed."

In the morning we went for round two. This time it was slow and gentle. With an easy rhythm, we reached our peak almost together. She went first and I followed soon after. It was warm and sweet, even loving. This was a turning point in our relationship. We got comfortable with each other. The tension had been released. We'd bared our souls to one another. We'd shared our bodies, intimately. As a result, the second week was a whole lot a fun, both in and out of bed.

Two nights before we were scheduled to return, we sat in the glow of the setting sun, cocktails in hand. Taylor had developed a nice beginner's tan, and her freckles were more prominent than ever. Her hair had developed a wild streak, so she pulled it into a ponytail that protruded from the back of one of my ball caps. We had salt on our skin and smiles on our faces.

"God, I love this place, Breeze," she said. "Thank you a hundred times over for this."

"My pleasure," I said. "Mind if I ask you a few questions?"

"Shoot," she answered. "Nothing can touch me out here."

"So you bribed a judge with my money, right? Does this happen often?

"You'd be surprised," she said. "Happens all the time."

"Have you ever taken a bribe?" I asked.

"I don't accept bribes," she answered. "I accept obscene amounts of money to keep criminals out of jail. Once in a while I defend an innocent person, but not often."

"So, you bribe judges, and you help people whom you know to be guilty go free. Do you ever have any problems with your own guilt? You know, do you feel worse about yourself because of what you do sometimes?"

"That's just it," she answered. "It's what I do. It's my job. That's how the system works. What are you getting at?"

"Would you agree that bribing judges is illegal?" I asked.

"Well, yes, of course it is," she answered. "But I've got to use every tool at my disposal in the best interests of my clients. It's against the law, but in South Florida its status quo."

I'd thought about this moment for the past few days. Taylor and I had gotten very close in a very short time. There was something left hanging that I wanted to get off my chest. I needed to come clean with her, but I wasn't sure how she'd react.

"I was running coke," I blurted out.

"Say what?" she asked.

"The whole time I was gone," I answered. "I was smuggling cocaine on this very boat. Now her holds are full of money, drug money."

"I figured as much," she said. "It sort of fits your modus operandi."

"Does that change anything between us?" I asked.

She gave me a mischievous look, clinked her glass to mine and answered my question.

"Running coke, bribing judges," she said. "It's all part of the game I guess."

"Like I told you before," I said. "It's all in the past now. I'll never do it again."

"Never say never," she answered. "You might need to be dangerous Breeze again someday."

"I'll have to find another way to stay sexy, if it comes to that."

"Shit Breeze," she said suddenly. "You slapped me with reality. What day is it? I have to go back to work."

"It's Thursday night," I replied. "We've got two days left."

"We'll have to make every minute count," she said. "Let's kick this party into overdrive."

And we did.

Life at Laishley

Back at Laishley Park Marina, Taylor put on her business attire and high heels. She brushed out her hair and applied makeup in an attempt to tame the newly highlighted freckles on her nose. I was sorry to see her preparing to return to the real world. I liked her before, but seeing another side of her out there at Cayo Costa made her even more appealing to me.

She picked up her bag and walked to the door. When she reached it, she stopped, sighed, and dropped the bag.

"I don't want to go," she said.

"You're more than welcome to stay," I told her.

"I've got some money," she offered. "We could just run away to the islands together and never come back."

"I've got some money too," I said. "That's kind of been a fantasy of mine."

"I wasn't serious. It's going to remain a fantasy, for me at least," she replied. "Breeze, you've helped me so much these past two weeks. I can't thank you enough, but the real world beckons. I've got a ton of stuff to do before Monday."

"I guess I'll hang here for a while, in case you change your mind."

"It will be good to know that you're around," she said. "But I'll be super busy for the foreseeable future. I feel great, thanks to you. I'm going back to that office ready to kick ass again."

"Maybe I'll hang a sign out front," I said. "Captain Breeze's two-week rehabilitation cruises. Pretty ladies de-stressed and loosened up, courtesy of sun, sand, and sex."

"You'll make a killing," she chuckled. "I'll write a testimonial."

I walked her up the gangway and out to the parking lot. Her heels clicked and clacked on the aluminum ramp leaving the docks. Alongside her car, she grabbed my shirt and pulled me in for a long, hard kiss.

"You're a dangerous man, Breeze," she said. "I've got to go, before I change my mind. You're like a drug. I just want more."

"You run along," I said. "I need a couple weeks to recover anyway."

"Give me a few weeks to get caught up," she said. "I'll be back."

"I really hope so, Taylor," I said. "But the choice is yours."

She drove off fast in an expensive looking Audi. She was a quality woman, much more high-class than I was accustomed to. She was smart and ambitious. I also found her extremely attractive. What the hell was she doing with the likes of me? *You still got it Breeze.*

There I was, alone in the marina with nothing to do. I decided to get to know my neighbors. Oregon Rod was still over on A-Dock, but he was preparing to leave on a cross-country camping trip. Jersey Tom had his boat at the end of B-Dock, but he had a job and wasn't around much. Bonnie had purchased a new boat since I'd been here last. She had it repainted and named it *Mother Ocean*. Clete was in the slip next to her aboard *Hey U*. Next to Rod was Mark, aboard a twenty-eight Carver. He'd gotten himself a pretty girlfriend. She lived up near Bradenton, and he spent a lot of time at her place.

Cheyenne was still around, but she'd dumped her boyfriend. Bruce didn't socialize much. Brad had just moved onto *Semper Fi*, two slips down from me. Tina and Herb had a completely refurbished Viking on the other side of me called *Mojito*. There was Mike and Lynn, and a Mike and Joan. There was an old-timer on a forty foot Pilgrim named Bob. I'd seen him and his dog out in Pelican Bay on occasion. He was pushing ninety, but still living aboard. The perpetual happy hour and open house was held nightly aboard Emoh, with hosts Harry and Karen. There was a moose and a kangaroo painted on the transom. He was from Maine, and she was from Australia.

I made the rounds to say hello and to introduce myself. Everyone was pleasant towards me, but it was clear that I was an outsider. I'd have to change that if I wanted to stay there. Socializing wasn't really one of my skills though. I'd been on my own for too long. The only real conversations I'd had were with Cross-Eyed John, and he'd be going to jail soon.

I kicked around the downtown area of Punta Gorda. I found a Tex-Mex place called Dean's. There was a Tiki Bar on the water behind the Sheraton, but it was kind of a tourist trap. Hurricane Charley's had good music most nights, but the food was hit or miss. All the places on Marion Street were upscale, white table cloth joints. I didn't feel comfortable going in alone. I felt most comfortable just sitting on my boat, drinking package goods.

I was pretty much stir-crazy after the first week. There had been no word from Taylor. The only thing I had to look forward to was the completion of my probation. Miranda knew where I was. There was no paperwork to sign or appointments to keep. When the day came, Miranda called and gave me the news.

"You're free, Breeze," she said. "It's over. You are free."

I took a bunch of beers over to Mark's boat. I sat with him and Rod and swapped lies for a couple hours. Bonnie stopped by to congratulate me. I got caught up on all the gossip, which I could have done without. Clete had broken up with Sandy. Joanie caught Rod kissing Bonnie. Julia had missed an invitation to a party and turned indignant on everyone. Tina and Herb went to Jamaica for a vacation. Karen and Harry left for Maine for ten days. It was all foreign to me. We all knew each other's business. It was like living in a trailer park some days.

Early one morning, I saw old Bob walking up the dock at his normal time, but the dog wasn't with him. He looked to be in distress. I threw a shirt on and went to see if he needed any help. He had tears in his eyes. His old dog had died during the night. He needed help with the body. He couldn't pick her up. I felt horrible for the man. He'd lost his wife years ago. That dog had been what kept him going. I helped him move her and we bagged her up. He had called someone to come and take her away. Together we carried her up the ramp and loaded her in the truck. He pulled out his wallet to pay the man, but I stopped him.

"Go ahead home, Bob," I said. "I'll take care of it."

He shuffled off with his head down. It was one of the saddest sights I'd ever seen. I had noticed some bad stains on his carpet from the dog. Later I got with Karen about renting one of those machines to clean it up for him. She and another lady had him over for a nice home-cooked meal to try to cheer him up.

The marina itself was an excellent facility. Rusty, the dockmaster, ran a tight ship. His assistant, Ray, was one of the nicest people I'd ever met. All the staff was helpful and friendly. They kept the place clean and running smoothly. I hated it.

I felt caged and constricted there. There were buildings all around. The noise was a continuous distraction. Cars and trucks crossed the bridge all day and night. There were lawn mowers, sirens, outboards from the boat ramp, and car alarms. I started getting the urge to go. I didn't have any destination in mind, but I had to feel free again. Only the thought of being with Taylor again held me back.

I tried hard to tame my wanderlust. I started re-doing all the teak on *Miss Leap*. It wasn't a labor intensive job, but the searing Florida sun made it a difficult endeavor. I'd be soaked in sweat in a matter of minutes. My beer consumption increased proportionately.

I was sitting alone one Friday night drinking beer, when I heard the click and clack of high heels on the dock. My heart rate increased and my stomach did a little flip flop thing. I knew it was her. She threw her shoes on deck and climbed aboard after them. I caught a quick peek of her panties as she threw a leg over the rail. They didn't stay on for long.

I rose to greet her and she shoved me inside.

"I'm real happy to see you," I said.

"No time to talk Mr. Dangerous," she replied. "I need you, right now."

"So much for small talk," was all I could say.

The lovemaking was frantic and hungry. It was hot, sweaty, and thoroughly satisfying for both of us. We moved together like a finely tuned machine. Afterwards, I lay there spent. She got up and started to dress.

"Have I just been the victim of a booty call?" I asked.

"Are you complaining?" she asked back.

"Of course not," I answered. "Stop by anytime. Maybe stay a while."

"I can't tonight," she said. "I just really needed you, but I have to run. You were awesome by the way. I've been thinking about you for weeks. I couldn't hold out any longer."

"No need to resist temptation," I said. "Captain Breeze's rehab shop is open twenty-four hours a day."

"I'll keep that in mind," she said, putting on her jacket. "Look, we need to talk, but I just don't have time tonight."

"It's never a good thing when a woman says we need to talk," I said.

"I'm sorry, Breeze," she began. "I've got exciting things going on, that don't involve you. I also have a proposition that you may be interested in."

"Now I'm curious," I said. "I'm getting itchy feet sitting in this marina. I could use some excitement."

"I'll try to come back this weekend," she said. "I really have to go now."

She gave me a deep kiss, like she'd done at the car that day. Breeze junior started to wake up, but she turned and left us just like that. I listened to click clack of her heels recede into the night.

I tried to make sense of the situation. She was obviously very busy with her career, but she'd taken thirty minutes away to get laid. I hadn't lost her completely. Exciting things were happening. They didn't involve me. She had a proposition for me. I couldn't even guess at what she meant by all that. I'd been happy that she showed up that night, but then I felt let down that she'd made a hit and run. I was not the one in charge of this relationship. Somehow, she'd manage to take control. I was left to sit and wait for her to make time for a quickie. That night, just after she'd left so hurriedly, I didn't think it would be enough to hold me. I couldn't see myself hanging around the marina, hoping she'd stop by for thirty minutes once a month.

I had a vague feeling of uneasiness about the whole situation. On the positive side, I was a free man. I had some money. I was involved with a desirable woman. I owed no debts. I wasn't running or hiding from a damn thing. On the negative side, I didn't really feel free. I was tied to a dock, living amongst other people. I wasn't out there on the water, enjoying nature. I'd allowed myself to be tamed. I lost the constant state of awareness that I'd lived with for over five years. I'd retired from the pirate business. My sole act of rebellion lately was peeing over the side after dark, instead of using the restrooms.

I'd have to lay down the law with Taylor. When she came back to talk, I'd tell her that we could be a couple, or I'd hightail it out of town. She was the only reason I came here in the first place. I was beginning to regret that decision, no matter how smart and sexy she was. The regret lasted two days. It was forgotten when she showed up on my finger pier with an overnight bag. She was not in her business attire.

"Would you like a little company, sailor?" she asked. "Sorry to be presumptuous, but I figured you'd be okay with me staying the night."

"Indeed, I would," I answered. "I can't think of anything I'd like more."

"Sorry about the other night," she apologized. "I was an ass. Forgive me?"

I folded like a cheap tent. I had a little speech planned for her return. I was going to lay it all on the line. I was going to firmly explain my thoughts and feelings about this affair. I did nothing of the kind. I forgave her and took her in my arms. She smelled like heaven.

"Welcome aboard, pretty lawyer lady," I said. "Please, make yourself at home."

"Thank you, captain," she said. "I have news."

I got each of us a beer and took her bag to the lower berth. We sat inside for privacy. She took a deep breath, and told me she'd been practicing her own speech.

"They're going to make me a partner," she started. "Since I returned from our vacation, I've been so focused. I'm a better lawyer than I've ever been. I resolved this and I took care of that. I brought more money to the firm in the last month than I did all of last year. I've been a machine, Breeze. I owe it all to you."

"Congratulations," I offered. "That's huge."

"They said I was too valuable to defend drug dealers in court," she laughed. "I thought of you."

"I'm glad I got caught when I did then," I said.

"They want me making deals in the office, and representing the firm," she told me. "They want to put me on billboards for Christ's sake."

"I knew you before you were famous," I said. "Mind if I brag about sleeping with the hot chick on the billboards?"

"Yea, that," she hesitated. "That's what we need to talk about."

"Uh oh," I said.

"Listen, Breeze. Please understand," she said. "I can't show up at black tie affairs with someone like you. Crap that sounded awful."

"I know what I am, Taylor," I said. "I don't like it much, but I think I understand where this is going."

"Do you?" she asked. "Because I don't. I don't want to lose you, but things are going to change between us. Slumming in a boat yard with a known boat bum would hurt my image. You have a criminal record."

"It's a marina, not a boat yard. And *Miss Leap* isn't just a boat. She's a yacht. You want me to play rich yachtsman?"

"I know you can't do that," she said. "You are what you are. It's one of the things that makes me like you, but I don't see a future for us."

"Weekend quickies?" I asked.

"If you can handle that," she said. "Friends with benefits could be fun."

Then I remembered how I'd felt after she left the last time. I dusted off the little speech I had planned. I told her that I was wasting away here, that I needed to move on. I couldn't stay here just for the occasional hump session. I felt caged. I wanted something to do to liven up my life. I missed living by my wits. I missed being on edge sometimes. I was getting soft and weak. I was becoming downright civilized, and I didn't like it.

"That's where my proposition comes in," she said. "Hear me out, okay."

I was curious, so I settled back and listened.

"The firm sometimes deals in special cases," she began. "We've been using PI's. They haven't been getting the kind of results that we hope for. I want to hire you, as a private contractor, when these cases present themselves."

"I'm no private investigator," I responded.

"You are a man of many talents," she said. "These cases I'm talking about, they call for a plan of action outside the law. Normal legal procedures have failed or exhausted themselves. We need someone who isn't the law, for that very reason."

"Okay," I said. "Now you have my attention."

The Case

Marlene Jones was seventy years old. She lived alone along the waterfront in a place called Lettuce Lake. She was quite wealthy. She had dedicated her later years to various charitable causes. She was by all accounts a kind and caring soul.

One day a boat had arrived in the waters behind her house. The man anchored within a short paddle of her property. Within a few days, he had introduced himself to Mrs. Jones. He was looking for odd jobs. He said he was handy with most household repairs, but would do anything for a few dollars. Marlene hired him to paint the wooden fence surrounding her lot.

He said his name was Max Gray. He worked diligently in the Florida sun. He was polite and well spoken. He was clean, showed no tattoos or scars, and spoke like an educated man. Marlene felt sorry for him. She befriended him, offering him more work when the fence was finished. They grew close quickly. She'd bring him cold sweet tea in the afternoons. They'd sit in the lanai and chat at the end of his work day. Eventually, she invented chores inside to keep him out of the afternoon heat.

He stayed on for a month. She was beginning to run out of jobs for him. She needed to attend to her assorted causes and club meetings. She assigned him one last task before leaving for an appointment. She trusted him.

When she returned, his boat was gone. When she noticed the vessel missing, she ran through the house inspecting valuables. Her jewelry was still there. Furs hung in the closet. The silver pieces were still in the hutch. He'd just left, knowing there was no more work to be done. He hadn't said goodbye, but it didn't look like he'd taken a thing. It took three days for her to remember.

She had a small lockbox in a special hiding place. It contained a sum of cash, but that was unimportant to Mrs. Jones. It also held several family heirlooms that she'd promised to her grandchildren. There was a diamond ring, a gold watch from her husband's retirement, and assorted mementos of her life. They were priceless to her. They could never be replaced. She hurried to the hiding place. Behind the bookshelf a false compartment was concealed by the heavy old tomes. She pulled the books out and opened the compartment. It was empty. The lockbox was gone. She cried for the lost heirlooms. She had trusted him, but he took her most valuable possessions. She cried for her lost faith in humanity.

The police couldn't do anything. His fingerprints were everywhere, because he had free reign of the house, with her permission. There was no proof that he'd stolen the box. They didn't even know if there ever was a box. They were unsympathetic to Mrs. Jones. She let a stranger come in and she all but deserved to be robbed.

Marlene had many connections throughout local society, due to her charitable work. She was an acquaintance of one of the partners at Taylor's firm. The partner referred her situation to Taylor. Now Taylor wanted me to recover the box and its contents. The guy lived on his boat. I was the perfect person for the job.

"Find him, Breeze," said Taylor. "Get her stuff back, and you can have whatever money is left."

"I need more information," I said. "What's he look like? What kind of boat? What color is it?"

"I'll meet with Mrs. Jones," she said. "Maybe you should come too."

"What if I can't find him?" I asked. "I'll have expenses."

"We'll cover expenses," she answered. "You can reimburse us if you make the recovery. If not, we'll eat it."

"Fair enough," I said. "I'll give it my best shot."

Marlene Jones was a sharp lady. She had short silver hair and a pleasant smile. Anyone could see that she'd been a knockout in her younger years. Her most striking feature was her obvious lack of breasts. She was a cancer survivor. It had spurred her into giving freely to others. There was fine pottery that she'd made herself, all over the house. She kept herself busy. Taylor introduced me and began asking Marlene questions about Max Gray.

Max was probably in his late forties. He had thick black hair with no beard or mustache. His face was round, with small ears and a prominent forehead. He was just short of six feet tall. Not overly muscular, but not skinny either. She said he had a thick build, but there was no flab. His hands were calloused and hard, with knobby knuckles. His eyes were a curious gray color.

The boat was an older Chris Craft, probably built in the seventies. She guessed it was a thirty footer. He'd built a canopy out of plywood and painted it gray. Although she had an attention to detail, she couldn't recall seeing a name on the boat. Maybe it didn't have one. From here, he could either go up or down the Peace River. If he went north, he'd run out of water soon enough. If he went south into Charlotte Harbor, he could be anywhere.

We thanked her for her time and prepared to leave. She stopped at the door and turned her attention to me.
"I just want my things back," she said. "I don't care if he goes to jail or not. I don't care about the money. I can't lose those memories. They're for my grandkids."
"I'll try, Mrs. Jones," I said. "I'll do my best."

Back in Taylor's car, I bounced a few ideas around. Going up river was a dead-end, but he could hide any number of places. I'd hire an airboat and make a quick scan of likely hideouts. Max had been gone for over a week. If he went south, it was hard to say where he might have gone. There weren't many coves to anchor in. I could cover Charlotte Harbor in a day or two, in my own boat. Once he made the coast, it was anybody's guess.
"I love how your mind works," said Taylor. "You would have made a great lawyer."
"And I thought you just wanted me for my body," I said.
"Speaking of that," she said. "Can you spare a girl twenty minutes?"

We only lasted fifteen, but it was enough. She dug her fingernails into my shoulders and shuddered beneath me. I hoped my slip neighbors didn't hear her sounds of pleasure. I hoped even more that they didn't hear mine.

She dressed quickly and headed for the door. I dismissed her apology and told her to go. I understood. At least, I said I did. It wasn't the time for regrets. It was time for thanks. She was an incredible woman. I was grateful for whatever time I could get.

Max Gray had not taken his boat up the Peace River. The airboat captain hadn't seen him, but we took a ride anyway. Dennis Kirk told me that no one knew this river as well as he did. If Max was hiding up there, he'd be found. I had to concentrate my efforts to the south. I left right away.

There were only a few boats anchored off the Punta Gorda waterfront. None of them was an old Chris Craft. I checked out the little bay near the Charlotte Harbor Beach Complex and saw nothing. I went up the Myakka River and struck out again. I cruised over to the mouth of Alligator Creek. He wasn't there. I got in close near Cape Haze and looked through binoculars at the holes in the mangroves there. I saw two houseboats, but no Max. I poked around Pine Island, Mondongo Island, and behind Useppa. I ran out of daylight without spotting him, so I settled down for the night in Pelican Bay.

I decided to head north the next day. The decision was made with the flip of a coin. He wasn't behind the golf course at Boca Grande. He wasn't in the Bayou behind the Pink Elephant. He wasn't anchored off Dog Island up at Placida either. I kept traveling north. I didn't see him near Stump Pass. It was early, but I decided to enter Chadwick Cove and call it quits for the day. There was a bunch of bridges to deal with further north. I didn't feel like the hassle.

There were several small sailboats to my port as I entered the cove. I had to go around a corner and make a hard left to find a spot to anchor. As soon as I made the turn back south, I saw the boat. It was anchored in an open spot in the south end of the cove. I dropped my anchor a hundred yards away. He didn't know me. He wouldn't know I was looking for him.

I settled in to watch and wait. He paddled out to his boat in the early evening, before dark. He was using a bright yellow kayak for transportation to and from shore. He stayed aboard for one hour. I watched as the freshly bathed and shaved man paddled back to the north and out of sight. The next day I watched again. He was not an early riser. He'd leave sometime around noon and paddle off. He came back at dinner time, got cleaned up, and headed back out. He stayed out until close to midnight.

I watched for three more days. The pattern remained the same. On day four, I went off in the direction he had gone. From previous experience, I knew that some of the local live-a-boards here used a restaurant called Flounders, to get to shore. It was at the end of one of the canals. The long-termers had figured out ways to get rid of trash, fill water jugs, and even park cars nearby. I drove my dinghy up the canal until I saw his kayak. I checked the bar but he wasn't there. I crossed the street to Englewood Beach and scanned the sunbathers. He was there, lying on a towel thirty yards up from the surf.

That night I tailed him again. He walked down the street from Flounders to the White Elephant. He took a seat at the bar. The bartender seemed to know him, or at least recognize him from previous visits. Max was living a life of leisure on his stolen money. All day he sunned himself on the beach. All night he drank in the bar. I'd seen enough. He'd be here for several more hours.

I got back in my dinghy but didn't return to my boat. Instead, I came alongside the old Chris Craft. I tied off with his boat between me and the homes on shore. It was quite dark. I felt relatively certain that I wasn't being watched. I climbed aboard and tried the rear door. It was secured with a padlock. I snuck around on deck. There was no hatch large enough for me to gain entry. I'd have to come back with tools. The wood around the door looked soft, possibly even rotten. I figured the screws would pull out easily.

I called it a night and returned to *Leap of Faith*. I waited. He returned near midnight as usual. The guy was an amateur. I'd learned long ago not to stick to a regular schedule. You never knew when someone might be watching you. You never knew when someone might want to steal from you. You didn't want to make it easy for them, by being gone at the same times every day. I paused to think about my upcoming theft. He'd taken valuable items, and cash, from a kind and generous soul. It hadn't really hurt her financially, but the sentimental things were important to her. She was wealthy and connected. Without her wealth and connections, she wouldn't have gotten to Taylor's firm. She wouldn't have me out here in the dark ready to steal her things back. Was I on the side of justice? I decided that I was doing the right thing. I wasn't stealing from the rich to give to the poor. In fact, it was just the opposite, but he was still a thief. He'd betrayed the trust she'd placed in him. He had set her up with a nice guy act, and robbed her. I didn't care what happened to him afterwards. I was just here to get the stuff back.

I felt good. There was excitement in the air. I was on a mission again. I had even convinced myself it was a righteous mission. It made me feel alive.

He stuck to his pattern the next night. I was ready. I took a small pry bar, a large flat screwdriver, and a hammer with me to his boat long after he left. I snuck aboard and attacked the hasp on the doorframe. It popped free with just a little effort. I took a quick look around. The lockbox wasn't just sitting out in the open for me to grab. The boat wasn't a big one though. There were only so many places it could be. I'd already broken in and damaged the door. There was no point in a careful search. I started rummaging through likely hiding places.

It took me almost an hour, but I found it. It was in the bottom of a box of assorted junk in the forward berth. The ring, watch, and other heirlooms were still in it. There was a bunch of cash. I quickly hopped back in my dinghy, taking the box and my tools with me. When I got to my boat, I realized I'd be a prime suspect when he returned. I could stay and bluff him. He probably wouldn't call the cops. If I left tonight, he'd know for sure it was me. He wouldn't know which way I went. He wouldn't return to Punta Gorda either. He'd have to think the police would be on the lookout for him. I decided to pull anchor and take off.

I ran all through the night, straight back for the marina. It was just like the old days, when I was constantly on the run. Hell, I enjoyed it. I was quite proud of myself. I'd found the guy. I'd recovered the goods. I'd avoided violence. It had been the perfect operation. Max Gray had been no match for Breeze. I found out later that he still had twenty thousand dollars of the money. I'd recovered thirty thousand. He could still live the good life, for a while.

When the adrenaline wore off, I slept for ten hours straight. When I realized where I was, it felt like a hangover. I was back to reality. I was back in the real world, with my slip neighbors, all the noise, and nothing else to do.

The Real World

I considered the money. The deal was, that I could keep it. I'd been gone less than a week. I'd burned a few hundred bucks in fuel. It seemed too much for such a simple job. Normally, I'd be thrilled to come into thirty grand, but I had plenty of money from smuggling coke. I didn't need it. Mrs. Jones didn't really need it either. I put five hundred in my wallet and put the rest back in the box.

"I've got it," I said to Taylor. "You'll need to return the box and its contents to Mrs. Jones."

"You have to come with me," she said. "She'll want to thank you in person."

"Pick me up," I said. "I want to talk to her anyway."

"I knew you'd come through," she said. "How'd it go? Any trouble?"

"Smooth as silk," I replied. "Piece of cake. Candy from a baby."

"You're amazing," she said. "I think you may have a new career."

Marlene's eyes lit up when we came in with the box. She seemed genuinely shocked to see it again. She opened it up to inspect the contents.

"Why is there cash in here?" she asked.

"It was no trouble at all," I answered. "I can't take your money. I recovered thirty grand. I kept five hundred for expenses."

"We made a deal, young man," she said sternly. "You will take the money."

I didn't want to argue with her, but I'd made up my mind. I'd done plenty of wrong in my lifetime. I didn't want to be rewarded for it. I wanted to do good for someone, for a change. I wanted to regain some honor.

"If you don't want the money," I said. "Give it to one of your charities."

"Excellent suggestion," she said. "It will do so much good. I didn't know what to expect from you Mr. Breeze. You're a little rough around the edges, but there's a spark of decency there. I can see what Taylor sees in you."

Taylor blushed and swore we were just friends and business associates.

"You can't fool an old bird like me," said Marlene. "You'd be in love with this man, if you'd only let yourself."

It was my turn to blush. I told you she was sharp. I changed the subject for both our sakes.

"If you see that boat back here, or if you see Max," I said. "Call the police."

"Thank you so much, both of you," she said. "Now run along. I've got a donation to arrange."

It had been a good couple of days. Marlene Jones was happy. Taylor was happy. I was happy. I was rewarded that night with a one-sided session in bed. Taylor made it all about me. I tried to reciprocate, but she would have none of it. I gave in to her administrations and simply enjoyed the moment. I wouldn't see her again for another month.

The law firm started an all-out advertising blitz with Taylor as the face of the company. The billboards went up. Her new duties kept her at the office twelve hours a day, seven days a week. Outside the office, there were dinners with clients, press functions, and the occasional court appearance. If I wanted to see her, I had to turn on the TV. Her commercials ran in heavy rotation. She answered questions on the courthouse steps. She was in the newspapers and on covers of magazines.

She had rocketed to stardom in the legal profession. She was the new queen of high society around Charlotte County. I felt pretty much forgotten. When she did call, it was to discuss another job for me. I completed the job successfully. I only saw her in person when I returned what I had recovered to her office. I never met the client.

Slowly, it all began to fall apart. She snapped at a reporter in an ugly exchange after a trial. She came off badly during a press conference. A senior partner nudged her aside and took over the questioning. She couldn't go out in public without being recognized. The newfound fame was wearing on her. The long hours were grinding her down. She was handling it better, and for longer, than I had, but she couldn't keep it up. Her work suffered. She made mistakes. The older partners turned on her. The younger partners had driven the path forward with aggressive tactics and a pretty face. The older men didn't like the results. Their practice had turned into a circus. It was now a reality show about lawyers, in their mind. The money was rolling in, but it was taking a toll on all of them.

There was nothing I could do about it. I couldn't even talk to her. I tried to busy myself, but it wasn't working. The boat was close to perfect. No maintenance items needed to be attended to. The teak was freshly finished and shining. Her fiberglass was waxed and her stainless was polished. I simply couldn't hang around much longer. I liked the work Taylor had given me, but she was gone. She wasn't living in another world, she was living in another universe.

She showed up at midnight with a fifth of Patron. Her hair was a mess. Her clothes were wrinkled and stained. There was no loving greeting. No hugs or kisses were given. She plopped down in a deck chair, kicked off her shoes, and took a big slug of the tequila.

"Can I just hide here for a few hours," she asked. "I left my phone in the car."

"Make yourself at home," I responded. "You okay?"

"I am not okay," she answered. "I thought I knew what I wanted. I had it all under control. Now it's all going to hell."

"I've been following somewhat," I said. "What I see on TV."

"That's not the half of it," she said. "The back biting and infighting behind the scenes is unreal. I think the firm is going to split up. There won't be a place for me on either side. They used me to start a power struggle. Now I'll be sacrificed."

She continued talking for another hour. I heard every sordid detail of the battle going on. Eventually, I stopped participating. I just sat and listened, while she carried on. I got up to take a leak. When I came back, she was asleep in the chair. The empty bottle of Patron lay at her feet. I left her there and went to bed. When I woke up, she was gone. She left a brief note.

I'm so sorry, Breeze. I haven't had time for you. My life is all fucked up and all I did was bitch and moan to you about it. You deserve better. Please forgive me. See you soon?

I didn't see her soon, except in the newspaper. Some intrepid reporter had made allegations of bribery in the south Florida legal system. Judges were implicated. Certain law firms were mentioned. Taylor's firm was one of them. With all the attention the firm had received lately, the press was drooling at the chance to take them down. They went after Taylor with a vengeance.

It was time for me to toss the lines. I didn't want to stick around and watch the vultures pick her bones. She was in deep trouble. The firm cracked in the middle of the investigation and threw her to the wolves. I hadn't heard from her since the late night tequila session. The younger partners broke off and started a new firm, claiming innocence. The old partners circled the wagons and prepared to defend themselves against any impropriety. I didn't know what happened to Taylor. She disappeared from the public eye. I didn't blame her. I'd have run away a long time ago, if I was in her shoes. Maybe she was made of sterner stuff than me. Maybe she had enough on the partners to keep her job. I didn't understand all the legal mumbo-jumbo, but I knew for a fact that she was guilty.

As soon as I came to that realization, something else dawned on me. What if I was implicated? Could they arrest me for bribing a judge? Of course they could. The investigation was just getting started. It was entirely possible that they'd discover my bribe, arranged by Taylor. That was the final straw. I had to get out of town. I had to go far, far away from this place.

I spent the next day loading essential supplies, groceries mostly. I'd made up my mind. I'd go to the islands alone. It wasn't the same as taking a beautiful woman along, but that part seemed like it would never work out. I wasn't getting any younger. The trail of women in my wake was getting longer.

I walked down the dock with a cart full of bottled water and canned goods. When I reached the boat, I found Taylor sitting on the aft deck.

"Looks like you're preparing for a trip," she said.

"As a matter of fact, I am," I replied.

"Where you going?" she asked.

"To the out islands," I said. "Far away."

"By yourself?" she asked.

"That's the plan," I answered.

"Change the plan," she said.

"How so?" I asked.

"Take me with you," she answered.

I was a bit overcome. I couldn't believe what I was hearing. The boat was all ready to go. I was ready to go. Now Taylor wanted to come with me? It was a dream I had chased for years. It didn't seem real. Before I could say another word, she took my hand and led me inside.

"First things first," she said. "Be sexy, dangerous Breeze for me."

I was happy to oblige. We made love right there on the salon floor. It was very good, and it felt very real.

It was no dream.

The outlaw boat bum and the embattled lawyer babe were sailing off into the sunset together.

The End

If you enjoyed this book, please leave a review at Amazon.com

This is the third book in a series. Make sure to read the first two:

> TRAWLER TRASH; CONFESSIONS OF A BOAT BUM
>
> FOLLOWING BREEZE

Cover photo by Ed Robinson
Cover design by Ebooklaunch.com
Interior formatting by Ebooklaunch.com
Proofreading by Karen Snow

OTHER BOOKS BY ED ROBINSON

LEAP OF FAITH; QUIT YOUR JOB AND LIVE ON A BOAT

POOP, BOOZE, AND BIKINIS

THE UNTOLD STORY OF KIM